An Arbiter's Gift
Matthew Wolf

Paperback ISBN: 978-1-62660-164-2

Cover and map art by Flavio Bolla
Author photo by Jamison Erwin
Book design: Michael Campbell

An
Arbiter's
Gift

Matthew Wolf

OTHER NOVELS BY MATTHEW WOLF

THE RONIN SAGA
The Knife's Edge
Citadel of Fire
Bastion of Sun
Tides of Fate

Short Stories in The Ronin Saga
Dreams of a Reaver
Visions of a Hidden
Legends
An Arbiter's Gift

To my fans. When busy roads grow quiet

(and books take too long to come out),

they still travel with me,

seeing greatness around the bend.

FARHAVEN

MEDIAN

Frizzian Coast

Kalvas Ocean

Ester

Wenceleas

WRKIW

The Dragons
Tooth

Mountains
of Soot

TROL

Kalvas Ocean

The Abyss

Death

FARHAVEN

The Abyss

Burai Mountains

Death's Gates

The White Plains

The

DE-GRAEL

Sobeku Plains

The Green Valley

Woonshire

The Lo

Koru Vil

The Silvas River

Lakewood

Burmen's Bank

THE LOS

DREKVAL

Dol

Himdel

Werkal Desert

The Gold Road

EASTERN KINGDOMS

The Crags

The Wastelands

Maiden's Mane

ops

An Arbiter's Gift

SITTING IN THE GRAND HALL of the library, Ezrah rubbed his tired eyes, trying anything to stay awake. *I need this*, he told himself, cramming at the last minute for his upcoming test. Unfortunately, he was falling asleep. His eyes scanned the tiny print, and his lids grew heavy. He pinched himself with a thread of flesh, but the alertness lasted only a moment.

Suddenly, his head hit the book, and he gave a loud, ripping snore, snapping awake.

All about the library, eyes bored into him.

Gray-robed Neophytes, like him, huddled over books. A girl with two stripes giggled, and Ezrah grew red-faced. *This isn't working.* Shutting the book, Ezrah rose, leaving the Library of Magic. He needed to get his mind off his failing studies, and took to the dusty streets. As he wove deeper into Farbs, the City of Fire, away from the black keep, his studies and worries seemed to fade. Ezrah grabbed a hunk of bread from a nearby cart and tossed a copper on the vendor's table when he saw a commotion in the bustling bazaar of Farbs.

A crowd stirred impatiently. Men, women, and children baking in the desert sun were waiting for water.

It was the Noon Water Giving.

Something churned inside him.

Pocketing his bread, Ezrah joined the jostling crowd, pushing his way through it. *Judging by the sun's height in the sky, the caravan should arrive any moment*, Ezrah thought. Stuck amid the mass of bodies, the air was hot, stifling. Sweat trickled down his temple, stinging his eyes. A surly voice rattled his bones, a husk gained from drinking, smoking, and a hard life. "Oi, you, what's a Neophyte doing in the streets of Farbs? Don't get enough water from your precious Patriarch, gotta steal ours, too?"

Looming in the corner of his vision was a big man with a wide face and dark stubble. Ezrah cursed and pulled his hood forward. *I should've worn different clothes.*

"Boy, I'm talking to you!" the rough voice said, and a fat finger jabbed Ezrah sharply between the shoulder blades.

"Leave him alone, Grimwal. He's just a child," said another in the crowd.

"Ain't none of them gray and red-robed bastards children. They ain't like us. Soon as they put on the robes, they become something else. Threaders," he cursed. "Your little spells, altering the elements and turning people into newts. That's all they do."

"We…can't turn people into newts," Ezrah muttered.

Grimwal leaned in closer, his breath rank. "What'd you say, boy? You think you're better than us, don't you?"

"Wait a minute," said another citizen, "can't Reavers conjure water from thin air?"

"You're right!" Grimwal boomed. "Oi, Neophyte, you little worm. Thread some water for us. You hear me?"

Ezrah sighed and spoke under his breath again, "It doesn't work like that."

He didn't intend for the words to be audible, but the brute had caught his low mumble. Ezrah's collar was yanked and he found himself face-to-face with the massive brute. At fourteen, Ezrah was small for his age, and this man looked the size of a draft horse. Grimwal's grimy vest strained against his barrel-like torso. Chest hair curled out from the top, dark and wild, glistening with sweat. A noxious smell issued from Grimwal's mouth like sour ale and month-old cheese. "Are you mocking me, boy?"

Others grumbled, telling Grimwal to drop him. The brute ignored their words.

Ezrah eyed the dirty fist gripping his robes, feeling his power well inside of him, yet he suppressed the desire and spoke calmly, "Not much water around us." He gestured to the burning sun above and the arid streets. "Only a Ronin can conjure something from thin air, and unless I look like a legend reborn…"

Just then, guards entered the square.

Their boots clanked, surrounding the citizens like a barrier of steel, protecting the precious water soon to arrive.

A guard pointed to Grimwal and Ezrah, hand on his sword. "You two! No fighting!"

"He's a stinking—" Grimwal began.

"I'll 'ave none of it!" the guard snarled. "Fight here, and I'll throw in the stocks thirsty and naked as the day you were born!"

Grimwal grumbled and let Ezrah go.

A moment later, Ezrah heard a familiar rattle and over the heads of citizens, heavy wagons rumbled into sight. The caravan had arrived. Immediately, the thirsty throng clamored for water. More guards followed, ringing the caravan, grizzled men and women with their hands ready at their hilts. Three carts, all bearing barrels full of water. Barrels that were more precious than gold.

"Outta the way!" a lean man with squinty eyes called, leading the caravan. "Seven hells, you mangy rats! Back off, or I'll trample you where you stand, and none of ya will get a drop!"

Fire and ash, Ezrah cursed inwardly. He recognized the man from when he was a child, begging for drops of water.

Mithas.

Mithas groveled at the Governor's feet and stepped on his own people to get a glimpse of his master's good fortune. Ezrah's blood went hot, remembering being kicked, beaten, pushed to the back of the line, and treated like refuse, all while Mithas had watched from his perch on the cart with a callous sneer upon his face.

An orange glow suffused Ezrah. The spark, magic.

No, he told himself, *wait.*

Ezrah's fingers gravitated towards a talisman in his pocket, a carved marking of the Devari symbol made from metal.

Calas, his mentor, had given it to him. Told him to grip the talisman when he was feeling lost or afraid. He had also taught him how to fight. Calas's deep words returned from memory, sounding in his head. *"Waiting for the perfect moment is an art and half the battle, young Ezrah."* So Ezrah breathed out, containing his ire. His gray Neophyte robes grew sticky against his skin from sweat as the people crowded closer, and he was jostled to the front.

A man with greasy dark hair and a long scar across his face yelled, "Step forth, say your name, and move on! Three seconds at the tap! Those are the rules! No complaining!" He said this as if on a loop.

Citizens clutched buckets, and guards poured from the barrels' spigots the allotted amount of water. A piddling amount. Always two carts, which left everyone just enough until the next day. As the water was doled out, the greasy-haired guard crossed names off a list.

Ezrah neared, pushing his cowl forward but still without a plan.

Moments passed by like hours. Water was doled out, and people bemoaned the meager amount when Mithas rose and put his ear to the casks, knocking and listening. Then he waved his hands and shouted, "That's it! No more!"

Ezrah felt as if he had been punched in the gut.

They'd only emptied the first cart's barrels.

There were still two more carts, barrels brimming with water.

Guards nearby gripped their swords tighter as if knowing this was coming.

4

A surge of outrage and shock welled from the crowd, and shouts rained from all about.

"You can't be serious!"

"We always get two carts! This isn't enough to live on!"

"My children are still thirsty," cried a woman.

Mithas licked his lips and shouted back, "Governor's orders to limit the rations! You've been getting more than enough for too long. Pay the fees, then you can have the second cart!"

A woman with a little boy cried back, "You can't do this! We can't live without the second cart!"

Mithas snarled, "That's not my concern." Then he looked to the guards, nodding, and the caravan surged forth, shoving its way through the crowds while shouts and cries followed them.

They tried to clamber up the cart, but guards pushed them off.

"Stop this madness!" Mithas shouted, shoving his heel at a young man trying to clamber up the cart. "Get off, you lousy—" Mithas's tirade was cut short as he was struck in the head with a stone. He wobbled, nearly falling off the cart's seat.

Guards shouted as well, wielding their swords. "Get back now, or we'll be forced to cut you down!"

Shouts and cries sounded for Mithas and for the governor's head.

Ezrah was caught amid the storm of outrage.

He had to do something and delved into his mind. There, in a field of black, was a little ember of orange. It was small, only a faint flicker. Still, he reached out, only for the flame to vanish. The cries all around him grew louder. An errant body shoved him. Ezrah was flung to the dusty earth. He tried to rise, and a boot caught him square in the teeth, splitting his lip. Blood filled his mouth. Dazed and looking through the tangle of bodies, he saw men and women rush forward to rip Mithas from the cart. Someone cried out as if stabbed by a guard.

Ezrah roared, trying to rise. The crowds stepped over him, pinning him to the earth, dust clogging his senses. He wasn't strong enough to get up. *Spark.* He needed his spark. If only he could thread. If only he was stronger. However, his senses fogged, and mind cloudy from the blow, his power was nowhere to be seen. More bloody cries. The fighting was escalating.

This is how it ends?

Helpless, just like back then.

The memory set a fire in his belly.

No. Not like this. He growled, biting an ankle pinning his arm. He had enough room to press up a little and shirk the foot off his back. Pulling in a breath, Ezrah delved inward, hunting for his spark. The field of black was still there. He breathed in, going deeper. In the distance, he spotted an orange flicker. *I can do this,* he thought, filled with a sudden feeling of hope. In the Citadel, he was weak, but out here, he *was* strong. Ezrah snatched the flame. This time, it didn't disappear, and he drew on its power. The faint flame became an inferno. The spark, his magic, grew. Twitching his fingers like puppet strings, he tweaked nerves in the nearest people. Muscles responded, and they moved aside. At the same time, hands grabbed him, helping him to his feet.

Ezrah saw Grimwal, the big man with a pudgy face and dark stubble.

Grimwal grumbled, "Stinking Neophyte or not, trampled to death ain't no way to go. Now, do you have a way to stop this madness?"

"I think so," Ezrah said with a small smile, wiping blood from his nose.

Mithas lay on the ground nearby, guards ringing him with steel.

Another dozen guards still held their ground before the last two carts.

Seeing Grimwal, hope filled him; and Ezrah threaded the element of sun. He focused it to a point. Smoke formed, and a hole was burned through the thick wood of a barrel. The barrel sprung a leak. All froze. He spread the points of light in the air. More holes, more leaks. People shouted in joy. Water poured into the street, and citizens rushed forward, filling bucket upon bucket. The guards, seeing it was a fruitless endeavor, picked Mithas from the dusty street and made a hasty retreat.

Grimwal gazed down at him. "Not bad, little man."

Ezrah grinned back. "Still hate Neophytes?"

"The lot of 'em," Grimwal grunted, crossing his arms. Then his sour expression twisted towards a smile. "But I'll make an exception for you. Go on now, get out of here before the guards come and find their little culprit."

Ezrah smiled, wiped his hands, and left the tumult of joyful citizens, their thirst now quenched. Turning a corner, he felt quite proud of himself when he felt a sharp pinch on his rear. Ezrah yelped, grabbing his backside, and turned to face his assailant.

Fera stood a dozen feet away, wearing a smug look.

"Fera…" he breathed.

Threads of flesh, he knew. That's how she'd pinched him from so far away. Fera was a master with flesh already. Her hands were on her hips, and her pretty heart-shaped face was wearing a look of amusement. Slim, Fera had dark hair and skin, like the color of coal, but darker, deeper. Many Farbians had her skin tone, but it was her eyes. They were bright purple, like shards of amethyst, a hue to make men and women gawk. It was said ancient Narimites from the Great Kingdom of Moon had eyes that color. Myths even claimed they could see better at night. It gave her an otherworldly air, but to Ezrah she was just Fera, his best friend. Though only fifteen, she was tall, not uncommon for girls her age, outpacing Ezrah by a good hand or two.

More passed, running to the square like a swarm of bees to honey. News of Ezrah's "good deed" was already spreading. Fera grabbed his arm, tugging him into a quieter dark side alley, away from the frenzy. "You're quite proud of yourself, aren't you?"

Ezrah smiled slyly, wiping the blood from his split lip. Crossing his arms and adding all the charm he could muster, he replied, "Ahem, I'm afraid I don't know what you're talking about. I'm always proud of myself. It's in my royal blood."

Royal blood. It was an inside joke. They were both as common as a housefly. She didn't rise to his charm and shot back, "That was a nice little trick you did there. Quite generous of you."

"Pft, you've no proof it was me."

She eyed him flatly. "I can see the sun threads still dangling in the air. Besides, what other fool would thread outside the Citadel?"

Ezrah grew serious. He peeked around the alley's corner to the jubilant citizens, then back to Fera. "They're dying of thirst out here, Fera. I couldn't just watch."

"You fool. Of course, I understand, but you're going to get yourself hurt. Even more." She grabbed his face and threaded a bit of flesh. "Is that better?

Ezrah touched his lip, feeling it was no longer split, now smooth and unblemished. He mumbled his thanks.

"Anyway, I'm not saying I wouldn't have done it. Perhaps that makes us both fools." Glancing around the corner, Fera eyed the four dozen streams of water pouring out of the casks. "Honestly, nice job. Not sure if I could have forked the element of sun into that many streams." A flicker of pride rose inside him at her praise. Coming from Fera, that meant a lot. For her age, Fera was one of the most talented ever to don the gray robes. In the Citadel, she was a prodigy.

Guards bearing the Farbian flame and no colors of the governor rushed by them, heading to the scene.

Fera pulled Ezrah back, deeper into the alley. "C'mon, we oughta get out of here. We can't be late." She tugged on his arm, turning.

Ezrah didn't follow.

She looked back at him, confused. Ezrah sighed. "What if I don't want to go back?"

She arched her brow. "Is the sun getting to you? Did you hit your head?"

"I'm serious, Fera."

"Why?"

"You know why." Ezrah turned towards the black keep in the distance that soared above the alley's walls. Four black pinnacles shot towards the sun, like obsidian claws seeking to grip and crush the orange orb if only to harness its power. "I'm failing in everything, Fera. I can barely light a candle while Reaver Sinistra or the other teachers are watching, but as soon as I'm away, the moment I'm in the streets —"

"— You're like a different person."

He let out a breath and slumped down on a nearby empty crate.

Fera sat next to him, resting her arm over his shoulders. "Maybe it's stress. Maybe you can't perform under the pressure of their eyes. Personally, I like the pressure, if only to rub it in their haughty faces each time. Yet Renalin, the Creator himself, knows that no one feels comfortable under Reaver Nalia's stare."

Ezrah shivered at the mention of Nalia. "I wish it was that simple. Only it's the same when I'm alone in my room. That?" He pointed back over his shoulder, indicating where the shouts and clamor still sounded, where casks were riddled with burnt holes. "That would've been impossible."

"Sometimes…" Fera lifted her hand, and a small flame roared to life, hovering in her palm, lighting the dim alley, "the smallest flame can become a raging inferno. You just have to find it inside of you. You'll figure it out. I know you will." She closed her hand, snuffing the flame.

"Maybe," he said, shrinking under her intense violet gaze.

"Or you won't," she agreed with a shrug, "and you'll be doomed to wander the streets as a hapless, sparkless, street urchin."

Ezrah groaned. "Thanks."

"C'mon," Fera said, rising. "I didn't come find you just to give you inspiration and a hard time. In case you forgot, *it's* today."

It. He hadn't forgotten.

Ezrah rubbed his already sweaty brow, feeling dread rise into the pit of his stomach. He felt suddenly sick.

Fera rammed the point home. "This is the last big test of the year, Ez. If you fail it—"

"—I'm banished from the Citadel. From learning magic. Yeah, you think I don't know that?"

She eyed their dank surroundings. "Well, hiding in the warrens of the city in some smelly alley isn't going to prevent that. Not taking the test means you fail. Better to try, right?"

"We're not all gods of the spark like you, Fera."

"Come now, if that was the case, I'd be a Reaver already."

"Or an Arbiter."

They both laughed. She teased, "Now I know you've lost your mind. We both know that takes a Grand Creation. C'mon." She grabbed him around the shoulder. "Reavers aren't the patient sort, and you can't run from destiny."

"Even if that destiny is awful?"

"Especially if it's awful. Just gotta make it different."

Ezrah let himself be tugged along, and as they walked, passing citizens and moving through the dry desert streets, his mind veered towards Fera's words.

A Grand Creation…

A Grand Creation was the single test it took to become an Arbiter. In a world of terrible power and incredible magic, Arbiters were the next thing to gods and Ronin. They could thread insurmountable amounts of elemental magic, for that's what it took to summon a Grand Creation. A creation that would serve a Great Kingdom and the world as a whole. As far as Ezrah knew, the Patriarch had made two Grand Creations. The Sunroad—a road that looked like glass inside the Great Kingdom of Sun, where light swirled beneath its surface. Miraculous, it fed mills and powered smithies. It provided light, warmth, and energy. He'd also created the Undying Light—a violet-blue light in Narim, Great Kingdom of Moon, that staved off decay and provided nourishment for those who dwelled beneath the surface. In a city that barely saw the sun, it was a godsend. That was the whole purpose of a Grand Creation. They were meant to last forever and fill a void of something essential that would alter all the world. It required enough power to create what a hundred Reavers working together could scarcely match.

The Patriarch was the last living Arbiter.

They made their way out of the desert warrens back to the Citadel, the black keep. Devari guarded the wide entry. Wearing the brown and black leather and chain that blended with the keep, Devari were legendary swordsmen who could use the ki, an ability to sense another person's emotions. For the full Devari, soulwed blades rested at their hips or on their backs. A faint sheen of red could be seen in their steel. Bloodstone—steel infused with a magical ore that gave it an eerie scarlet hue and allowed Devari to dissolve spells of magic from thin air. They were the guardians of the city. Others were unnerved by the Devari, but Ezrah rather liked them, their brooding expressions and quiet stalking, like stone sentinels of men.

They moved through the gates into a courtyard, up the stairs, and into the hallways. These were swarming with messengers and servants in orange livery and gray-robed Neophytes. Neophytes like Ezrah and Fera were acolytes of the spark, beginner threaders of magic. Special boys and girls, some even full-grown adults, were all training to attain the coveted title of Reaver, a master of magic. A familiar voice called out, "Young Ezrah!"

Ezrah turned to see Calas, the leader of the Devari. His heart buoyed like a bubble of air in the depths of the ocean. Calas was sturdy with deep caramel skin, shaggy hair pulled back in a single long komai braid, a broom-like moustache, and a face that looked like the bluff side of a cliff. It was Calas who had found Ezrah so many years ago. He'd taken Ezrah under his wing, pushing him to test for the spark and join the Citadel, claiming there was spark in every man and woman. In the years following, Calas had become a mentor. Now, while Ezrah had never had the nerve to say it, Calas was like the father he'd never had.

Grinning, Ezrah ran and embraced his friend, trying and failing to wrap his arms around the man's muscled brick of a body.

Calas laughed heartily. "My goodness, young Ez. You're getting too strong for your own good. You've got the brace of a Cerabul."

Ezrah let go, feeling suddenly sheepish. All his carefully cultivated cool demeanor vanished when he saw Calas. Then and only then, he felt his youth. None of the strings of formality, the ties of power, the pressure to be a small god of the spark. He was just 'young Ezrah.'

Calas gave a polite nod to Fera. "My lady Fera."

Fera straightened her back as if the looming Devari didn't dwarf her. "I'm not a lady, Calas. Neophyte Fera is more than adequate. I'm not yet a Reaver. If another heard you saying that, it would be most unfortunate."

Calas waved a hand, smiling warmly. "Soon enough, my lady, soon enough." Her brows drew down, and Ezrah expected a tongue-lashing, but Calas didn't give her time to respond. "Off to the test?"

Ezrah groaned.

Calas slapped him on the back with a chuckle. "What a brave face. I hope that's not the face you make when you enter battle."

"If by battle you mean lighting candles, juggling rocks, or scrubbing dishes, then yes. That's all we ever seem to do," Ezrah grumbled.

"Ah, then you'll be happy about today. I hear Reaver Sinistra has cooked up something clever for your final test."

"What is it?" Ezrah asked, grabbing at Calas's leather vambrace.

Fera tsked. "Ezrah!"

"What?" he pressed, keeping his voice low. "If I can know even a little tip or trick to get ahead, perhaps I won't be…how did you say it? A hapless, sparkless, street urchin? C'mon, Fera, it's not cheating, it's just a head start. Right, Calas?"

Calas stroked his moustache, looking amused. "You do have such a way with words, my young friend."

Fera growled, looking about as denizens of the Citadel passed them in the black hall as if they might have overheard. "Don't encourage him, Calas. Ez, you know that's strictly against the rules." Fera shook her finger at Calas. "Devari chum or not, you'll get him kicked out before he even gives it a shot."

Calas waved his hands disarmingly with a good-natured smile. "Easy, easy there, my lady."

Ezrah pressed, "Just a *hint?*"

"Afraid not," Calas sighed. "It is against Citadel law. Besides, getting you in trouble would wound me deeper than an Algasi spear. I'd never forgive myself."

Ezrah slumped.

Calas leaned in, grinning. "I can tell you, however, that it'll give you goosebumps."

"Calas!" Fera griped.

Calas only laughed and slapped Ezrah on the back. "I suggest you hurry. Good luck!"

Ezrah grinned. "Goosebumps… So it's a test of flesh."

Fera snagged his arm, dragging him along, grumbling as they went. "Calas is a fool, telling us that. He'll get himself in trouble with the Patriarch, let alone Reaver Nalia."

Ezrah shivered at Nalia's name again. "Bah. Knowing the element we are using gives us no advantage. Except for you." Ezrah was awful at manipulating threads of flesh. It was often considered the most dangerous of the elements, as many spells of flesh were forbidden.

Fera, however, was a natural. She could use Truth Speech by the time she was only ten—a spell to make people say things they didn't intend to say, speaking their truth. Flesh had many uses, though. Pinching nerves, moving muscle, sinew, tendon; all were the domain of flesh. It was said that the Ronin of Flesh—if the Ronin weren't myth—could reanimate the dead. It was rumored he had made the Drekkars, Balrots, and other beasts and could change his flesh to look like anyone. Unfortunately, Ezrah couldn't do much more than cause a mild muscle spasm, and sometimes, it was his own. Taking a deep breath, they moved through the halls, and he rubbed at the metal talisman in his pocket for reassurance.

They reached the wide silver doors and heard voices inside the room.

12

The test had already begun.

"We're late!" Fera exclaimed.

Ezrah pushed the door open a second before Fera. Inside was a large room with vaulted ceilings and wood crossbeams. On the walls, light orbs glowed. Above, a chandelier hung from the center, hovering over the students' heads, bearing dozens of candles, each lit an ominous red to mark the coming test. Eyes fell upon him and Fera, a hundred Neophytes in gray robes. They sat at dark wood desks, two per table. To their immediate right, standing at the head of the class, was Reaver Sinistra.

Reaver Sinistra was a square brick of a woman with a tight bun of gray hair. A pair of spectacles always sat too low on her nose. She'd only push them back up when she was really mad. Her ice-blue eyes had the annoying trait of freezing a person where they stood. At that moment, it happened to be Ezrah and Fera. "Good of you to join us, *Neophyte Ezrah, Neophyte Fera.*" Her thin smile faded. "Ten-point 13 deduction for tardiness."

Fera opened her mouth, a squawk of protest.

Reaver Sinistra cut her short. "To your stations. You are holding up the rest of us."

Ezrah dragged Fera to an open table near the far wall.

An older Neophyte with four stripes, a big man, came forward and put a square container covered with a black cloth before him, then another before Fera. It rattled. *A cage.* Other four-stripe Neophytes distributed the cloth-covered cages to each student.

Ezrah reached out, drawn to the cage.

"Do not touch!" Reaver Sinistra snapped.

He shrank back.

Fera rolled her eyes as if saying, *'C'mon, Ez. Get it together.'*

He grumbled but stuffed his hands in his robe pockets.

Reaver Sinistra rubbed her brow, trying to contain her frustration. "You are all being given your test as we speak. Once they are all handed out, I will explain, and you will begin."

"Don't look now, but we're next to your favorite person," Fera whispered suddenly, nudging him.

Ezrah glanced to his right. *Ah, seven hells,* he cursed inwardly.

Neophyte Logan. His two other brothers were nearby, but Ezrah avoided their stares. Their father was a shoo-in for the next Arbiter, and he'd groomed his three sons to all be nearly as insufferable as him.

Logan, handsome and annoyingly talented, believed he was Renalin the Creator's gift to Farhaven. He had bright blue eyes and dark hair parted to the left, with a single curl that rested on his forehead. Ezrah hated that little dark curl as Logan thought it charming and boyish enough to offset his unbearable personality. Logan was predictable to a fault, as were his insults. Upon seeing Ezrah, Logan's mouth worked as if conjuring one.

Three.

Two.

"'Bout time you showed up, hog's breath," Logan sneered, low enough that Reaver Sinistra couldn't hear. "Just because you're an orphaned rat doesn't mean you have to smell like one."

A few of Logan's cronies snickered nearby.

"Ignore him," Fera said under her breath.

Ezrah was way ahead of Fera. It took more than a few petty words to rile him. Calas's wisdom echoed in his ears as they always did. *Wait for the right time.*

Reaver Sinistra was at the head of the room and chastising another young Neophyte who was trying to glimpse beneath the black cloth.

Logan leaned closer. "What? Too afraid to speak?"

"He's scared," said another Neophyte crony of his, a girl with a violet streak in her jet-black hair.

Logan huffed. "Course he is. Can't thread more than a trickle, isn't that right? *Orphan rat.* You're a pretender. A fake."

Fera, at his side, rose up. He saw the fire in her eyes, and a light orange mist disappeared off her fist. She had spark welling inside her, ready to lash out at Logan and his sycophants. Just like in the city with the casks, Ezrah wouldn't let this get out of hand. He put his hand on Fera's. He gave her a light shake of his head. The look in his eyes said everything: not worth it. She grumbled, sitting back down, and Logan and his cohort cackled. "Your girlfriend won't always protect you, you—"

Suddenly, out of a sliver of shadow, Reaver Nalia appeared as if stepping out of an invisible doorway.

The element of moon, Ezrah knew.

Other students sat wide-eyed.

Nalia was a presence, a force. Four stripes on her cuff. She was powerful, strong, and something more… Something that terrified Ezrah. Her looks only seemed to accentuate her aura of power. Nalia wore the standard scarlet red robes of a Reaver that matched her wild red hair. Her face was boney, with a sharp nose, overly protruding cheekbones, and narrow-angled jaw, tilted eyes. She was alluring, only the gauntness gave her a hollow look, her features too refined and sharp. According to rumors, Nalia's hunger for knowledge left her hunched over books for days on end, forgetting such necessities as food and drink.

Nalia snapped a finger, and Logan sat upright in his chair, muscles strained as if on the point of snapping. Reaver Nalia leaned over Logan, her eyes on fire as if having heard the whole exchange. "Careful, little toad. Do not belittle the power of friendship when you have none." Nalia's scarlet robes were close enough to touch. He saw her four stripes, and he wanted to reach out and touch them, though he knew it was like yearning to touch the glittering scales of a serpent. A bite was sure to follow.

Logan was still leaning forward in his chair, frozen stiff.

"Reaver Nalia," Reaver Sinistra said, looking frazzled upon Nalia's sudden entrance. Sinistra bowed her head deeply. It was the difference between a three-stripe and a four-stripe. "I—I—" she stammered, "I didn't expect you. I thought the Patriarch had need of you."

Reaver Nalia twiddled her fingers, and Logan gasped a breath. She sighed. "Alas, our Patriarch is a busy man, my dear sister. I am, like you, only a humble servant."

"Ah, yes," Reaver Sinistra said as if searching for words. All the students were rooted, listening. "May we help you?"

"You mean why am I here? The truth is, I heard this was a promising class with some remarkable potential. I came to observe. However, I see some of your students are not taking the test seriously."

Reaver Sinistra's eyes fell on Ezrah, who, despite himself, was smiling. Of course, it was purely because of Logan's reaction. The fool had been full of arrogance, and now he looked ready to soil himself, a switch that had happened in a matter of moments. Reaver Sinistra

15

fumed, "I see. Neophyte Ezrah, this is the last time your insolence will go unpunished. Do not fear, Reaver Nalia. I will see to it personally."

Ezrah felt the fire of anger and opened his mouth to protest.

Reaver Nalia spoke for him, wagging a finger. "Not him. Him." Her eyes flickered to Logan. "This one was the culprit."

Reaver Sinistra's arm shook as she gestured to the door. "*Out*, Logan. I will deal with you later."

Reaver Nalia held up a hand, stalling the order. "No. He stays. I wish to see their merits. Afterward, I will personally escort them to the Headmistress who will mete out a proper punishment…" Then, as if realizing she was ordering Reaver Sinistra about like a scullery maid, Nalia smiled thinly. "If this is acceptable? This is your class, after all."

Reaver Sinistra swallowed, finally inclining her head. "Yes, that seems fair."

"Perfect. Then you may proceed with your instructions." Nalia moved to stand against the wall, studying the students like a hawk. It seemed strange that she had showed up so suddenly. A few times, Ezrah felt her eyes pass with more scrutiny over their table. Was she watching him? Or Fera? Her eyes made Ezrah's skin crawl. A hunger in her gaze. Was that his imagination?

Reaver Sinistra took an even breath. "Your test is this. Inside, you will find a maze and a mouse. You must guide your mouse through the maze to the center using only threads of flesh. You will be judged by how quickly you can accomplish this feat."

Logan nudged his nearby friends, a dark light in his eyes.

Ezrah knew that look.

Reaver Sinistra saw it, too, and her spark glowed about her. "I should not have to put words to this, but you must not harm your mouse. Threads aptly applied will only control its muscles. We are protectors of life in all its forms, not destroyers."

"What if we do…harm it?" asked another nervous Neophyte across the room. "Not intentionally, mind you, but sometimes flesh is hard to control."

Reaver Sinistra answered, "If you tweak too hard on tendon or bone, and your mouse suffers? A forfeit of the test, young Neophyte. I suggest you thread wisely."

Ezrah snickered. Good. Logan was annoyingly talented—not like Fera, of course—but he used his spark like a cattle prod. Even then, Ezrah was the weakest one here. He stared at the black cloth, his palms growing clammy.

"You have one minute to prepare your minds," Reaver Sinistra said, and her fingers danced. A globe of sun appeared in the air, slowly fading—a typical marker of time. When it was extinguished, the test would begin.

Ezrah took a deep breath and watched as other Neophytes closed their eyes, focusing their minds.

To thread was to channel the element, which meant embracing what the element represents. For fire, it was anger; water, going with the flow, and so forth. For flesh, however, it was embracing and being "inside" your own body. Feeling your skin, your heartbeat, then imagining the other creature's heart, skin, tendons. *The more you can connect with yourself, the more you can connect to another creature. That is the essence of flesh.'* Those were the words the Reavers drilled into his head. Unfortunately, Ezrah was always in his own head, not his body. He breathed in, trying to feel his own heartbeat. He felt it, but all he could think about was Nalia's eyes, Logan's smirk, and how if he didn't accomplish this, he could be thrown onto the streets.

A light ruddy aura began to glow around a few of the students' hands.

Even Logan had a faint sheen over his fingers.

Ezrah growled. Staring at the black cloth, he felt nothing.

Fera put her hand on his shoulder and whispered, "Relax, you've got this."

She didn't need the time to prepare.

He whispered back, "Easy for you to say. Flesh is your strongest element. It's my weakest, Fera."

Fera winced. "Uh, you're not so great at water either."

Ezrah groaned, rubbing his brow, feeling it was as sweaty as his hands. "You're really helping."

"Sorry. I'll shut up."

Heart hammering, Ezrah looked up and saw the globe of sun hanging in the air. Abruptly, it winked out.

"Begin!" Reaver Sinistra ordered.

17

Ezrah's heart leapt. He, along with every other Neophyte, ripped off the black cloths covering their cages. Sure enough, inside was just as Reaver Sinistra had described, a maze and a mouse. The maze was an eight-pointed star made of colored wood like a rainbow, the Star of Magha. It represented all the nine elements, aside from the banished element of wind. Tucked in one corner was a little mouse, fast asleep.

Why did I get the sleepy one?

"Alright, little guy, time to wake up."

Ezrah delved into his own mind, and in a field of black, his spark waited, a tiny flame as he always imagined it. Usually, it was hard to find inside the walls of the Citadel, but there it was. *Maybe I can do this…* Ezrah gripped it, letting it fill him. He opened his eyes to see a ruddy pink glow about his hands. He grinned. The mouse had awoken and now gazed up at him as if he was a titan. *Titan.* That struck a chord and a memory, and words returned. Calas's voice in his head.

18 *It's not about your size, it's about your heart, and in that, you're a titan.* Ezrah looked again at the mouse. It was smaller than the others. Just like him. It seemed only fitting. "Let's do this… You and me, Titan, nice and easy…"

Ezrah breathed in and tried to imagine he was inside the mouse's body. He could feel Titan's small heart hammering, the muscle and sinew, down to his tiny bones. Ezrah's fingers danced, and pink threads of flesh wove their way through the air and into Titan.

The mouse moved a small paw forward. Then another.

The finish line was in his vision, zig-zagging towards the center.

I'm doing it!

Together, they moved down the first corridor, then the next, avoiding several dead ends, heading towards the center. Out of the orange point, towards the green, then blue. It was like puppeteering, only Ezrah imagined *he* was moving through the maze. *You got this, little guy. Hells, we got this. Seven hells, what if we won? What if we're first?* He was never first. As this thought ventured into his head, a voice yelled out.

"Done!"

There were gasps from all around. Ezrah's concentration slipped, returning to the desk, to the room filled with Neophytes and Fera beside him. Inside Fera's cage, her mouse sat on the tiny star in the center. Finished.

Others stood on chairs or crowded closer to catch a glimpse. *"No way. It can't be,"* others whispered.

One of them exclaimed, *"Done already?"*

"She cheated!"

How? Even Ezrah felt a sense of disbelief. He knew Fera was talented, but this? It felt like it had only been moments...

Reaver Sinistra approached from a distance, pushing her way through the sudden clustering of small gray-robed boys and girls, her voice like a whip. "Enough! What has gotten into you all today! Out of the way this instant! You are clearly mistaken; she couldn't possibly have—" Reaver Sinistra's words fell short as she pushed aside those last few Neophytes. Her hand covered her gaping mouth. "Neophyte Fera..."

"My lady Reaver." Fera bowed her head, but Ezrah could see she was hiding a smile.

"I stand corrected. I..." She floundered for words. "This...has to be the fastest time the maze was ever completed in the history of the Citadel." Sinistra's wrinkles deepened at the corner of her eyes. "You are a true prodigy, girl."

Ezrah saw over the heads to Reaver Nalia, who watched with a slight smile, a glimmer in her eyes.

Reaver Sinistra placed a strip of black cloth next to Fera. Fera eyed it in awe. Her fourth stripe. While it would be sewn on later, it was a mark which they had been dreaming about. A hairsbreadth from the coveted title of Reaver. Reaver Sinistra rounded on the nearby Neophytes. "Well? What are the rest of you gawking at? Time is running out! Back to your mazes, quickly now, lest you prefer the dusty streets of the city over the Citadel."

Those gawking few, including Ezrah, shook themselves and returned to their tests, though most had already done so, feverishly racing to get their mouse across the finish line next, to the center of the Star. Fera and he exchanged smiles before Ezrah dove back into Titan's mind...and yet... A lingering thought clung to him like a cobweb. *How can anyone be that good?* It took all his effort just to get the little mouse past the first three points. Fera had navigated all eight points. *Her success is not your failure,* he reminded himself. *Focus.*

Fera echoed this, cheering him on. "C'mon, Ez. You got this. Just breathe, concentrate."

"Right," he replied, and he delved inward. The spark waited, and he gripped it. It filled him. "One step at a time."

Eyes bored into him.

Fera's. Nalia's. Sinistra's.

Block it all out. Concentrate.

His threads of magic moved across the distance, towards the little mouse once more. To most untrained, it would look like nothing, but to the trained, they were reddish-pink strands of light, connecting him to the mouse like a puppeteer's strings.

The mouse moved.

Until he tweaked a muscle too hard. Titan spooked and dashed left, racing towards a dead end. Annoyed, he tried to ply the little mouse back with another muscle twitch, urging it the other way. Titan continued to claw at the dead end. "Titan, c'mon, that's not the way…"

Ezrah had more inside of him. He knew he did.

Feeling failure loom, Ezrah's hands glowed a deeper ruddy red. *I can't fail.* What he was doing wasn't working. However, threads of flesh were like a surgeon's scalpel, and if he wasn't careful…his power would go beyond him. He fed more into the ephemeral pink strands, and the light tug became a yank. Titan squeaked. A flush of worry flooded through Ezrah. "No, I…" He tried tugging lightly again. However, the current of power in him—like a funnel already opened too wide— gushed outward, and he tweaked the leg so hard he feared Titan's limb would break. Titan's resulting squeal was awful. Ezrah dissolved the threads immediately, and the little mouse scrambled to a corner. Titan stayed there, shivering as if trying to curl up into a ball and not be seen.

"Ez…" Fera said over his shoulder. "You can stop. You don't have to…"

Tears welled in his eyes. He tuned her out. No, Fera was wrong. He needed to finish. If he failed, his chances of staying in the Citadel… This was his last chance. He reached out, his palms growing ruddy again. Titan shivered harder as if knowing what was coming. *I have to,* he thought. *I'm sorry, little guy.*

"Finished!" Logan called.

20

Ezrah glanced to his right. Logan's mouse sat in the center of the maze. Logan wore a smug look. "Thought you'd be better at this, seeing as you're related, orphan rat."

Fera rose, moving to stand between him and Logan, glaring. She said something that made Logan flinch, and the boy shrank under Fera's violet gaze, grumbling something.

Ezrah ignored them both.

He pulled more power.

He couldn't let Logan win, couldn't fail here.

Titan was shivering when memories assaulted Ezrah. They came in flashes.

He was suddenly transported back. Ezrah stood, watching in horror as bandits raided his small hometown, a little desert oasis on the outskirts of Farbs. He was six years old, an orphan. Anna, his mother's best friend and his last living protector, huddled closer to him as the bandits looted and burned everything he knew. Fires roared.

They ran, and all about, men and women were beaten, corralled.

Anna grabbed his arm, and they fled.

They ran through burning houses, pushing past the cobbler's home into a back alley. "If we can get to the outskirts, we'll be safe," Anna said. "I think Madara's camel is still at the town's southern well. Just stay by my side."

Ezrah said nothing, too scared to speak.

They reached the outskirts, and sure enough, there was the old broken well and the camel. Anna put him on the aging camel's hump. She smiled, brushing a tear from his cheek. Screams sounded in the distance, and his eyes flickered up. "Don't listen to that. Go now, Ezrah." The reins barely fit in his small hands, hands that couldn't stop trembling. "Don't stop for anything." She reached to slap the rump of the camel when a bandit, a gaunt-faced man, appeared. He pulled Ezrah off the camel, sending him sprawling to the dust, and his world rocked from the pain of it. Looking up, Ezrah saw the brute snatch Anna's arm and throw her down, pinning her against the broken well.

"Clever girl, but there's no running. Can't have you warning other towns or those red-robed bastards." Then he turned, looming over Ezrah. He blocked out the sun. Ezrah felt terror to his bones.

Ezrah was frozen, shivering. Just like Titan.

21

The gaunt-faced man raised his dagger.

He could do nothing.

He was weak and useless.

Why am I so weak? If only I was stronger…

Ezrah suddenly returned to the moment. He pushed the horrid images down where they remained buried and focused back on the task at hand.

At a nearby table, another student let out a moan. "Mistress! I think… I think it's dead… I killed it…"

Almost immediately, the spark in Ezrah's mind fled back into the dark recesses. Titan remained in the blue corner, five points away from finishing.

Then he remembered something from before, still sitting in his robe's pocket. The hunk of bread from the market. Ezrah pinched a crumb of it, then he tucked the bread under the fold of his thumb to hide it and held his hand over the maze—but not inside. This drew a wary, raised brow from Reaver Sinistra, but she didn't stop him. She moved to a nearby table to confirm another Neophyte had passed. At least half of the room had finished. There were hardly any left still trying. Ezrah breathed out and whispered, "C'mon, little guy." He waved the bread before the mouse, and its little nose twitched, following. As it did, he began to guide it, quicker and quicker.

"You're doing it!" Fera exclaimed.

Ezrah moved past each colored point, closer to the center, closer to the finish line.

There must have been only a dozen or so students left because he saw others gathering around him. More whispers. "Are they going to pass? Ezrah or Winifred?"

They must have been the last ones.

"Ezrah is behind, but he's catching up!" said another Neophyte.

There was no time to spare a second glance, and Ezrah moved his hands, his fingers fiddling as he pretended to thread.

Whispers echoed around him from other Neophytes, doubt and confusion heavy in the air.

"I don't understand. I can't even see his threads," said one.

"You dolt," whispered another, "that's because they're so subtle and complex."

22

"You're wrong," Logan said. "I can see them. They're basic and small."

He ignored them, moving Titan. Left, right, forward, until—

His mouse found the center.

"Ezrah passes!" a student exclaimed.

Reaver Sinistra appeared, her matronly features shedding much of her doubt as she smiled down at him. "I knew you could do it. Well done."

"Very impressive, indeed," Nalia added, appearing from nowhere like a dark shadow. Then she turned over his hand and revealed the bread. "For a cheater." She looked down at him, and while he wanted to shout that he had to, that he couldn't kill the little mouse, and he was afraid of his own power, his mouth went dry instead.

Neophytes gasped. A swirl of whispers and shock followed, palpable enough to make Ezrah feel sick. Only one face mattered, though.

He turned to Fera, who was at his side. She took a small step back, shaking her head slightly as if confused.

"I... I had to," Ezrah said. "I couldn't kill it."

Reaver Sinistra intruded, her face red as Sevian wine. "Neophyte Ezrah! You know the rules. Cheating is strictly forbidden upon penalty of banishment." Then her anger waned to disappointment. "I thought I saw potential in you, something more... That's why I pushed you so much harder. I suppose I was wrong." She crossed her arms and looked away. "Go to the Headmistress at once. "

Reaver Nalia stepped forward, and a quirk came to her lips. "Reaver Sinistra, if you will... Allow me to take him."

Ezrah shook his head. Something about Nalia was all off. She scared him more than the Headmistress. "I can go on my own."

"No," Reaver Sinistra said, "I can't trust you. Nalia will escort you. For now..." She raised her hands, and fire issued forth, little strings of orange in the air. As it did, cloth stripes were burned from Ezrah's robes, like moths had eaten up his sleeves. "You are demoted. Go, child. Leave my sight."

Ezrah choked a breath, staggering back, eyeing his burnt sleeves. He would rather the flames eat away his skin.

Years of hard work, Ezrah thought, *all gone.*

Neophytes had gathered in a throng about the tables, some keeping their distance as if afraid to get nearer, while others crowded closer,

23

staring and whispering, mostly in horror. Burning the stripes almost never happened. Ezrah looked up from his burnt sleeves, seeing Fera's expression. Sadness and disappointment.

"Come along, Ezrah," Reaver Nalia said with a flick of her fingers. Not Neophyte Ezrah. Just Ezrah. He supposed, in a way, he would have to get used to that. For now, he just felt empty as he followed Nalia. She suddenly paused, and her red robes whirled as she looked back. "Join us, will you, Neophyte Fera? I have someone who would very much like to meet you."

Fera swallowed, looking about at the other Neophytes as if Reaver Nalia had misspoken. "Me, my lady Reaver?"

"Yes, you. You're the child prodigy, after all."

"Who am I to meet, mistress?"

"Someone important who you should have met long ago," she said cryptically and turned.

24   Ezrah had no choice but to follow with the hot glares of others on his back.

"*Banished…*" he heard them whisper.

The world was a blur about Ezrah as he pushed open the doors and followed Reaver Nalia down the black stone corridors. The halls were quiet, only a scattering of Neophytes, Reavers, and Devari.

Fera moved at his side, silent.

He needed to say something, to break the awkward tension. "Fera, I'm sorry, I…"

"You don't need to apologize to me, Ez."

Scratching his head, Ezrah chuckled despite his situation, or perhaps in spite of it. "Uh… Why do I get the distinct feeling that I do?"

Fera eyed him, brows furrowed. "It's not me you're letting down, Ez."

A pair of young girls wearing the gray Neophyte robes passed. They gawked at his frayed cuffs. He shot them glares, trying to cover them, but he didn't care about a bunch of gossiping girls. Not when he was being dragged to what felt like the headsman's axe. "Because I cheated? Fera, I had to…"

"That's not it. This isn't right." She had tears in her eyes. "This isn't you."

He felt as if she was throwing another rock on him when he was already being buried by an avalanche. Anger swelled inside of him. "Don't you get it, Fera? Maybe this *is* me. Maybe I'm not right for the Citadel. Maybe I've never been cut out for this. Maybe I don't belong here. I'm different from you."

Fera rounded on him. The sudden fury in her expression and trembling body doused his own anger like a deluge of water on a flickering flame. "That's a pile of dung, Ez, and you know it! The truth is you're afraid. You've *always* been afraid. Not of your weakness, but of your strength. *That's* why I'm sad, because you...you can be so much more. You can be the best of us. Instead, you keep yourself small. You're given the keys to a kingdom, to a world of potential, and you throw it away. Now it's landed us here." She bit her lip, looking away.

Ezrah opened his mouth to protest as they turned a familiar corner to find Reaver Nalia straight-backed, her slender, spider-like hands clasped before her. "This is where we part, young Ezrah. It's a shame, really, how different two lives can be." She looked to Fera. "One destined to change the world, and another..." she eyed him, "destined for nothing."

She snapped her fingers, and the metal and wood door opened. Inside was a row of chairs, and in them, petulant Neophytes, a group of boys Ezrah knew were prone to causing mischief, sat against the wall. Behind a thick wood desk of silveroot sat a clerk. Upon seeing Reaver Nalia and her four stripes, the waiting Neophytes gawked. The clerk leapt to his feet and began to stammer a greeting. Nalia cut him off. "I've another for the Headmistress."

"Yes, my Reaver. What was the boy's transgression?"

"Cheating," she said, glancing at his singed cuffs.

A collection of wide eyes from the young boys in the chairs.

Ezrah hung his head.

"I see," the clerk said, eyeing Ezrah shrewdly. "Very well. Take a seat, young man. The Headmistress will see you shortly."

Nalia bowed her head. "And Ezrah? Be honest about your transgressions with the Headmistress, or it'll go much worse for you." Nalia turned to Fera. "Neophyte Fera? Shall we? *Destiny* waits for no one." Her dark gleam returned. The way she said it... Ezrah didn't have the ki, the ability to sense others' emotions, but there was something off.

What was it, though? Was it just his imagination?

His train of thought was interrupted as Fera gave him a sad smile and followed Reaver Nalia. Ezrah couldn't let it end this way. He reached out, snatching Fera's wrist. "Fera, I couldn't kill that mouse. I couldn't do it."

Fera's violet eyes looked at him as if he was missing something so important. She gave a small shake of her head. "You wouldn't have killed it, Ez."

"You don't know that."

"I do, and you do too."

"Will…" he summoned his voice, frail and thin as it was, letting the words and his fear out, "will I see you again?"

She rushed forward and hugged him tightly, her fingers digging into his back as if she didn't want to let go. Nalia cleared her throat impatiently, and Fera pulled away, wiping her cheeks and hiding her tear-streaked face. As she pulled away, Ezrah took out the metal fragment, the Devari insignia carved into the talisman, the one Calas had given him. He slipped it into Fera's gray-robed pocket as she turned and left, walking down the long corridor.

Thoughts churned inside of him. *What did she mean? How did she know I wouldn't have killed it?* And afraid of his own power? Ezrah wasn't afraid of anything. Though immediately, the words were a lie in his own mind. Somehow, he knew she was right, but he was afraid to admit the truth.

"Shut the door and take a seat," the clerk insisted. He must have said it a few times because this time was louder and vexed, clearly annoyed.

Ezrah wanted to rebel, wanted to fight, but he didn't. He slumped into a chair, feeling dazed.

The clerk sighed, rolling his eyes at his half-filled instruction. "Fool boy. Can't follow simple instructions. No wonder you're destined for the streets."

Ezrah didn't care. The words were just chatter. He sat there, lost in his own thoughts, despair draping about his shoulders like a heavy blanket. He knew what was coming. The Headmistress would arrive, hear what he had done, and he would be banished from the Citadel. Perhaps right there on the spot. Soon, this would no longer be his home. A sense of resignation settled into his bones.

26

It's what he deserved. He was weak, after all.

And yet… There was something off in Nalia's final words. The other students beside him murmured, eyeing his burnt and frayed cuffs. He didn't care. Something was all wrong about this. Something he couldn't put his finger on.

He turned to the three boys—dirty blond fourteen-year-old identical twins, Aiden and Caiden, and their older brother, Yumar, who was huge for his age as if he could be their father. He'd seen them around the Citadel, always getting into trouble, almost as much as him. Ahead, the clerk buried his head into a ledger, scribbling loudly with a quill, muttering to himself. Ezrah lowered his voice. "Say, can you three do me a favor?"

All three looked at him as if he was crazy.

Caiden opened his mouth.

"Don't talk to him, Caiden," Aiden snapped, jabbing him with an elbow and picking his nose. "Cheating on a test for a stripe? He's a dead man walking. We don't consort with the dead." 27

Ezrah scratched his jaw and gave a wry smile. "Then how about considering it a dying man's last wish?"

The group sat in a tense silence for a while.

Caiden repeatedly opened his mouth. Each time, Aiden shook his head or glared at him.

"Please," Ezrah begged.

The bigger brother, Yumar, spoke. "What do you want us to do?"

"Yumar!" Aiden whispered hotly in protest.

"Bah," Yumar said, "you two are always proposing half-baked ideas and making me move the heavy things or pretend to be the adult. Where has that ever landed us?"

"I…"

"Right," Yumar said. "So pipe down, Aiden. I'm going to hear what Ezrah has to say. Go ahead. What do you want help with? And why should we dig ourselves a deeper hole?"

Ezrah's hands tightened into fists. "I can't stay here. Something is wrong. Fera… I think she's in trouble. If you can create a little distraction, I can sneak out. Just a little mischief. Nothing that's going to net you more than a stern tongue from Headmistress Charlotte."

Yumar scratched his jaw. "I'm in." He looked to Caiden, who grinned and nodded emphatically.

All three turned to Aiden, who crossed his arms across his chest. "Well, now you're all thick as thieves, you don't need my help. Besides, all we did was steal sweetcakes from the kitchens. I'm not suffering any worse fate for Ezrah's folly."

"We need you," Caiden said. "You're the brains."

Aiden grumbled, looking away, and Ezrah saw he was growing red in the cheeks.

"Besides," Ezrah added, knowing Aiden was on the fence. He decided to sweeten the pot, "I promise to get you a date with Fera."

Aiden's eyes narrowed. "You're lying."

"No, really, she's always fancied you."

"Bah, fine!" They whispered to each other conspiratorially for a moment, then nodded.

"You'll get your moment. Use it wisely. Help Fera."

28

Ezrah grinned. "Perfect. Distract the clerk for a moment, that's all."

The boys were on their feet. Without pause, as if well-practiced in these sorts of shenanigans, Yumar picked up Aiden and threw him across the marble floor, leaping upon him. Then Caiden joined in until it was a tussle just out of sight of the door. "You're dead!" Aiden spouted, casting water, and Yumar patted it aside with a bout of fire.

They were fighting, and the clerk dove into the fray as they took the fight away from the door. They rolled, smashing into the thick desk, sending papers showering into the air like snow. The clerk shouted, trying to break it up. "What is this nonsense? Stop it right this instant! I said, stop it!"

Ezrah opened the door, out of sight of the commotion, and slipped back into the hallway. He knew he was just exchanging an immediate punishment for a delayed and even greater one, but there was something off about Reaver Nalia. There always had been, really, but now, it made his skin crawl. The look in her eye, that dark gleam.

Destiny waits for no one. That's what she had told Fera.

Perhaps she was taking her to see the Patriarch? Yet why hadn't she said that? Worse, Ezrah all this time had thought Reaver Nalia had been interested in him, but it was Fera with whom she had been infatuated. To what end?

At the same time, what if it was just his imagination? Was he following them only to land himself in deeper trouble? Then he chuckled. What else could they do? But his mirth fell short there. Reavers, adept with the spark. There were worse fates than banishment. Especially from Reaver Nalia.

Ezrah growled, shaking his head, pushing through the halls, past denizens of the Citadel, moving faster. It didn't matter. For Fera, he'd face the fire of the Seven Hells of Remwar. He had no idea where they were going, but he followed the metal talisman he'd slipped into her pocket. He was attuned to it. He had touched it and knew its every snaking line, and now the metal was like a part of him. He reached out in his mind, moving through the corridors, sifting until he felt it. The talisman was like a glowing light that shifted back and forth as Fera walked. Grinning, Ezrah followed, taking a hard left.

He came to a crowded four-way intersection and suddenly spotted Calas amid a group of Devari, coming closer. Decked in dark chain- 29 mail and leathers, they were intimidating. They moved gracefully, purposefully like stalking wolves.

A surge of emotions churned inside of Ezrah.

Seeing Calas, he felt joy. He wanted to run and tell the man everything. Calas could help him. Yet what would Calas think? Calas was a stickler for the rules and for duty. Sure, he'd given Ezrah a hint for the test of flesh, but that hadn't held any weight. This was different. There's no way he'd approve of Ezrah shirking his fate from the Headmistress to track Fera on some half-cooked notion of Nalia's questionable intentions. Worse, Ezrah had cheated and was soon to be banished. He felt sick with guilt. Calas's look of disappointment might just kill him.

Calas's keen eyes surveyed his surroundings for trouble, but fortunately for Ezrah, the hall was crowded with other Neophytes. Ezrah used it to his advantage. He dipped behind a pair of chatting Neophytes, his gray robes blending. Then, pulling his hood far forward, he brushed past his friend, moving down the hall. Towards Fera. The Citadel's warrens ran north, south, east, and west, extending to all parts of the city. He knew the Citadel tunnels were extensive, but they were ancient relics, used only as passageways for fighting during the ancient war. As Ezrah moved further from the dark keep, he knew he was likely under the desert streets of Farbs proper. He imagined those above, clamoring for water, baking under the relentless sun.

He heard a faint trickle now and again. It was said there were aqueducts beneath the ground, reservoirs of water sloshing beneath the city. Reavers had tried to pull the water out to supply the people dying of thirst, but the aqueducts were too deep. Too far. This had led many to believe the water beneath the city was only a myth.

A *worry for another time*, he thought, shoving it down and pressing on.

In his mind, the orange glow from the metal talisman moved faster, drawing him deeper.

Fera and Nalia were quickening their pace. Why?

Worried, Ezrah hastened his pace as well.

There were few if any denizens of the Citadel down here. To his knowledge, the keep's depths held only old storage rooms. Rooms that were filled with old magical tools, furniture, or armor from the days of ancient wars. Still, the talisman led him deeper and deeper.

Suddenly, he came to a dead end.

No...not a dead end.

He felt it. The talisman *was* beyond that wall, fainter now through the thick barrier of stone, yet it was undeniably there.

Ezrah opened his mind to the spark and felt the differences in the stones, the cracks and seams. Over one stone, in particular, Ezrah saw a web of gray light like magical cobwebs. It seemed like a hidden spell, only to Ezrah it was clear as day.

Ezrah reached out and pressed it.

The stone sunk in, grating as it did. As soon as the stone sunk in fully, the other stones began to shift, turning this way and that. They rearranged themselves to create an ever-widening hole. When the stones finished shifting, it was a perfect archway that revealed a dimly lit corridor beyond. Ezrah's jaw ground so hard it hurt. Fera was waiting, and for that reason alone, he stepped inside.

As soon as he did, the many stones magically shifted and shut behind him with a thunk. It was a wall once more. His mouth went dry. Darkness enveloped him. Ezrah was suddenly blind. His breathing quickened. He reached for the talisman in his pocket, forgetting it wasn't there. Calmly, he opened his mind to the spark. Delving inward, he found his spark and drew out threads of fire. Fire was always his strength, the opposite of water. It required rage only and no temperance, and he had plenty of that to spare. Ezrah threaded the glowing filaments of orange into a bright flame that lit the cramped walls and hallway a dozen paces ahead. On the walls to either side, he saw two brackets where torches were missing. He smelled pitch. Ezrah's skin no longer tingled with a sense of unease; it crawled as if covered in insects.

Summoning a breath, he followed, faster now. After another turn, he was led to a spiral staircase with faint red light, as if winding into the beating heart of the Citadel. It ended at a stone door with a pattern of nine elements.

The metal talisman was beyond.

Ezrah tugged on a heavy brass handle, but it didn't shift. Lifting the fire closer, Ezrah examined the elemental pattern closer.

The Star of Magha.

Each pin from left to right of the star was colored to match an element—blue, green, red, yellow, orange, purple, brown, black, and white. Stone grooves showed they could slide along the channels to be positioned at different points of the star. Ezrah noticed, however, the elements weren't lined up in proper order. An old child's rhyme returned to him, called "The Balance of the Elements:"

> *Air it flows, winds, and snakes,*
> *Light it burns, scorches, and creates,*
> *Leaf it binds, finds, and cultivates,*
> *Water crushes, erodes, and even slakes,*
> *Fire and flame, it burns and roars,*
> *Darkness and shadow, hides, ignores,*
> *Earth it sunders, shatters, quakes,*
> *Blood and bone, blunders, and breaks,*
> *Metal and soot, melds, binds, and flakes.*

He slid the pins into different positions on the star, arranging them from most powerful to least based on the poem. Air it flows... Wind. Light it burns... Sun. He whispered the poem aloud and mimicked it in the Star's pattern. Wind, sun, leaf, water, fire, moon, stone, flesh, and metal. So that meant... White, yellow, green, blue, orange, purple, brown, red, and black. When the black metal pin slid into place with a deep click, Ezrah grinned. He pulled on the brass handle. It turned, and he leapt inside. As he moved through the threshold, Ezrah's skin pricked as if magic was touching him, stepping through an invisible barrier. He pushed aside the strange feeling and moved through a huge hallway flanked by torches.

As he turned a corner, his heart dropped.

"Seven hells…"

A staircase, each step wide enough for a wagon to roll on, lay before Ezrah. Enormous pillars ran the length of the room made of black marble. They reached towards the ceiling, each wide enough that a dozen men with arms linked would have barely touched fingertips. The vast chamber itself could have fit a sprawling town.

It was lit with torches all the way up to a soaring ceiling that scraped the streets of Farbs. It seemed an errant foot from a citizen above could poke through at any moment. But the size of the chamber wasn't what made his blood run cold.

In the center of the chamber was a gigantic maze, just like the one he had navigated with his little mouse. It stretched into the distance. While he couldn't see all parts of it, the star had nine points—not eight like Ezrah had been used to, trained to believe was the only way, all his life. Each point of the giant star was a different color, but not painted. It was alive with the element. In the orange section of the maze, flames danced along the walls. *Fire.* In the blue, thick cerulean fog obscured the path, though Ezrah could see shards of wicked ice coating the walls. *Water.* Leaf, in the far distance, was a tangle of vine and root, metal for metal, and so forth. Even wind. A white haze obscured the mysterious heart of the maze. It had pitfalls and traps and dead ends, and all of these were alive with the elements. The maze was a death-trap: terrifying and awe-inducing all at the same time.

At the bottom of the stairs, he saw them.

Reaver Nalia and Fera.

Every muscle tensed.

They both were facing away from him. Nalia's flame red hair seemed to draw the fire's light. Her slender fingers were white-knuckled as she gripped a fistful of Fera's hair. Fera was pressed to her knees, facing the maze. Then he saw it, a collar around Fera's neck of red metal. *Blood-stone.* It negated the spark. Fera couldn't thread. Something came over

Ezrah, and the spark roared to life in his mind. Fire coalesced into a molten orb, and he flung it, sending a huge fireball towards Nalia.

Nalia lifted a hand without even turning. A sphere of water formed, and the fire collided, turning to hot mist. Nalia sighed, glancing over her shoulder, her bright pink lips twisting in a smile. "What do we have here? It seems a little mouse has snuck into our maze and interrupted our conversation. Careful, little mouse. You don't want to hit your friend, do you?"

Fera's head whipped around, and her face flashed with emotions—first shock, then elation, and at last, dread. "Ezrah! How…" She shook her head. "It doesn't matter. You have to flee! Nalia's mad! Run, Ez! Please!"

"Fat chance," Ezrah said to Fera. He was shaking, though he tried to cover it. Tried to let his anger rise up and consume the terror he felt for Nalia and the dark gleam in her gaze. "Let her go, Nalia. *Now.*"

"Or else what, child?" Nalia asked, amused. She eyed his frayed burnt cuffs. "You aren't even a Neophyte anymore. I am a four-stripe Reaver. A legend. A god in the eyes of the pathetic rabble above."

33

"A demon!" Ezrah shouted back. "They fear you, they don't respect you. They don't respect us." He remembered their looks, the citizens' looks, and the words of Grimwal. "We can be more. We should be more." The words sounded like Fera. "We can use our spark to aid the people. To save them. Instead, you create fear in order to control the people." He understood—all of it was out of their own fear. They felt small and needed to exert their power on others. Just like Nalia. She was the worst, twisted by power.

Fera's eyes shone, looking up at him as if she saw something in him, something unexpected.

Nalia's lip curled with a dark smile. "A pretty speech, little mouse. But the truth is simple. You and them," she said, eyeing the ceiling as if seeing the citizens, "are fated for the same thing. A pitiful, meaningless existence. Your friend, on the other hand…she might be more."

"Ez, run! Please! You—"

Nalia yanked on Fera's hair, cutting her short. Ezrah's anger flared. "Shhh, my little prodigy. Your dear Ezrah is now a witness to the trial of a four-stripe. The Great Maze." Then she tsked. "Shame, it's forbidden now. The Patriarch believes it is a barbaric practice. I suppose since it has killed nine out of every ten Reavers who've entered. However, I passed, and so can she." Nalia's eyes blazed with that strange dark gleam. "Before you came, I was having difficulty convincing our prodigy here of her potential. I admire her fire. Thankfully, now that you've arrived, I think I have the proper incentive."

Ruddy pinkish threads formed in the air above Nalia's hand, and Ezrah took an unconscious step back.

"Ezrah!" Fera cried out.

Nalia flung a hand, and Ezrah saw filaments of red jettison through the air. He leapt to the side behind a pillar, but more red threads followed. He tried to burn them out of the air with fire, only for the threads to dash through his flames. His fire was too weak for Nalia's potent magic. The spell sank into his bones. He felt his arms and legs moving without his command.

Nalia waved a hand, and Ezrah was flung, or more accurately, he leapt, though not of his own will, down the marble stairs. He tumbled, bones bruising, flesh hitting the hard marble edges until he lay in a crumpled heap. "Get up!" Nalia cried.

Again, threads plied his muscles to move. He was on his knees, gritting his teeth against it.

Move, damn it! Break the threads! If only he could move his hands, could summon fire, water, flesh, anything, but Nalia's fingers danced, moving him like a puppet. "Do me a favor, will you?" Nalia's eyes flared, and her grin grew wide and horrible, showing rows of perfect teeth. "Kill yourself."

Despite every fiber of his being, Ezrah's hands gripped his chin and the back of his head. He began to twist. He tried to rebel, but it was useless. Tears leaked from his eyes.

Fera shrieked. "Stop it! Please!"

Nalia continued to speak as if it was all a curious game. "It's amazing, really. While flesh is often viewed as the weakest element, we can contort anything against its will. Even beyond its own limits. I've forced a man to rip the muscle from his biceps by lifting a boulder the size of a wine cask. This should be an easy task for you." Ezrah's neck craned, turning more and more, and he cried out. His muscles ached, pulling harder. His spine twisted, straining farther, as if his neck would snap like a brittle twig at any moment.

In the corner of his vision, he saw Fera snag something at Nalia's waist.

Nalia cried out.

The threads of flesh binding Ezrah abruptly dropped, and he slumped, catching himself with shaking arms. When he looked up, Fera held Nalia's ruby-colored dagger in both hands. It shook in her hands as she pointed the dagger at Nalia.

Nalia smiled, gripping her own arm. Blood dripped down her hand. "Very resourceful. I'm going to make you regret that." She clapped a hand, and Fera was sent to the ground, shaking and convulsing from a wave of threads of flesh, stabbing her nerves. "Flesh is fascinating; it doesn't even have to be pain to feel like pain."

"Enough! You're killing her," Ezrah shouted, crying.

Slowly, Nalia stopped. "I suppose you're right. The mind can only handle so much, and I need her fresh for the trials ahead."

Ezrah's voice was hoarse, his power drained. "Why are you doing this?"

Nalia turned to him, neck craning. Fera continued to breathe heavily on the ground. "Why? Why did they torture me? Why does the owl eat the mouse? The answer is simple. Because it's our destiny. However, you are peculiar. There's something about you that feels… off. You must have some spell or incantation around you that I can't see, some sort of protection. That must be how you passed the barrier."

"What barrier?" Ezrah asked.

"A barrier that only Reavers can pass, or those bearing bloodstone, like your little friend. Still, you are just a pest." She raised her hands to finish him.

Ezrah didn't have the strength to fight. However, he would die on his feet.

Fera rose, blood dripping from her nose. "Enough… Please… I'll obey… I'll go into your stupid deathtrap. Just don't hurt Ezrah. Swear you won't harm him anymore."

Nalia smiled indulgently. "Deal."

The words were too familiar, too close to another. *Anna.* The memory seared his mind. Ezrah shook it off, pushing it back down, and called out, "Fera, no! You don't have to do this."

Ezrah's knees buckled, and his wrists snapped together before him as if he wore shackles.

"Oh, but she does," Nalia said, then stepped forward and removed her bloodstone collar. "Go on, girl, quickly now, and I'll spare your lion cub. If you succeed, you'll be my right-hand pet. If you fail… well… Then we'll know you aren't as special as I thought. Either way, your destiny is revealed."

Fera moved towards the huge maze, towards the first point, which had the sheen of orange on its walls. He called out to her, but she ignored him. She stood before the maze. The first opening was a wall of flame.

His voice was hoarse. "Fera…please…" Tears were streaming down his face.

She smiled, looking only at Ezrah. "Don't be afraid, Ez." Then Fera erected a barrier of water and stepped inside.

36   Nalia wiped her hands. "Well, it seems there's no more use for you," she said as soon as Fera was gone. "Goodbye, little anomaly." She sent out torrents of fire. Ezrah fought back with water. Water was never his true strength, but he had to try something different. As he did, he felt something beneath the surface of his thoughts, tucked away, something swelling. He roared, but Nalia's fire was too much. It seared away more of his robes, eating away, burning his skin. He knew he was going to die. He didn't fear his end—only he heard Fera's voice as a memory.

You're destined for so much more.

She was wrong, and he felt sorrow. Not for him, but for Fera, alone in that maze.

The flames ate higher, burning, scorching, stealing his breath. His right arm turned red, searing away skin. His thin barrier of water evaporated. His shield was gone. The fire roared forth, engulfing.

As soon as it did, the magic vanished.

Ezrah collapsed, and arms caught him before lowering him down gently.

He looked up to see Calas's gruff smile. "Calas? What in the seven hells?"

Calas growled, moustache twitching. "What did I tell you about cursing, boy?"

Nalia stood, hands on her slender hips, dark hair swaying. Her mouth soured. "Of course. Calas. The boy's savior and right hand." She eyed Ezrah on the ground disdainfully. "You've just the dumb luck to have a Devari as a guardian."

"Nalia." Calas raised his Devari blade. It glowed with bloodstone. The gem could cut the magic from the air. That was how he got through the barrier Nalia mentioned. Nalia's eyes tightened, clearly wary of her new opponent. "This is madness. What reason could you possibly have to hurt innocent children?"

"I could say the same. From where I'm standing, your logic is just as flawed. What reason is there to foster the weak?" she said, looking towards Ezrah.

"Because he has something you don't. Heart…and sanity."

Nalia's full lips twisted in a sour expression. "How touching. However, I'm not some fool child in gray robes playing at being a hero. You're still not enough to face me, Devari. You have to know that, don't you? I didn't get these by accident." She wagged her scarlet cuffs and their four black stripes.

"We'll see," Calas said.

Ezrah groaned, trying to sit up, and Calas pushed him back down. "Calas, Fera is—"

"In the maze, I know. I'll save her. It's all right, boy. You've done well. Rest now. I'll handle it from here." Ezrah felt his body slacken. In a daze, he threaded water to cool his burned arm, and it made a blue and red swirl.

Calas rose, turning to face Nalia.

Fire danced in her palms, and Ezrah saw a sheen about her. It emanated off her body like orange steam. Spark. Enough to rival a dozen Reavers or to level a hillside. Without warning, she screamed and sent out a river of fire. Calas lifted his sword. The inferno roared about him, most of it seeming to funnel towards the blade in his hands. Then the fire was gone, absorbed into the weapon, the steel glowing red like an ember from the fire.

They danced back and forth, exchanging blows. Nalia sent a barrage of elements. Calas cut the threads. Nalia ducked and dodged slices by erecting shields of stone or ice. Both parties separated then lunged back in a terrible dance of death. Ezrah witnessed it only out of the

37

corner of his eye. As soon as he felt he could move, he staggered to his feet and made his way towards the maze and the wall of fire, trying not to catch Nalia's attention.

Calas cried out.

Ezrah looked over to see Calas. He wiped blood from his nose, and scorch marks marred his leather and chain. He was on one knee, and Nalia was grinning.

"Calas!" Ezrah called.

"I'm fine, boy. Go save Fera. Now."

"I can't leave you."

"You have to. I've got this. I'll hold her off."

Ezrah exchanged a look with Calas, staring into the man's soul, and knew he meant it. Voice raw, Ezrah called back, "I'll come back for you. I swear it." With that, he turned, tearing himself away. He ran towards the maze's opening, towards the wall of fire.

Nalia roared. "Don't you dare help her!" She sent a spike of ice, and Ezrah barely ducked it. The ice smashed into the wall of the maze, shattering into a thousand shards. As he neared the maze's fiery entrance, he summoned moisture out of the air, forming a thin veneer of water around himself. He leapt through the fire. Flames surrounded him, and the thin barrier of water evaporated. He rolled and came to his feet, patting his clothes that smoldered. His body felt hot, but he wasn't burned any more.

The skin on his right arm, while still blistered, was healing. Though it was pink and raw in some areas, the wound had closed as if knitting itself back together. How?

He pushed the question down.

Deal with your immediate surroundings, the wisdom of Calas instructed.

Looking about, Ezrah took in every little detail, calculating his next move. The maze walls were shades of living orange, fire imbued inside. He sent out a bout of fire, and the wall only pulsed with energy.

No use… Somehow the wall nullified his magic.

The orange walls and floor danced like flames, beckoning him.

Fera was beyond in the bowels of the treacherous maze, and Ezrah started forward. As he took the next corner of the star, flames leapt out from beneath him. He rolled left and right, barely dodging them.

The ground cracked and split. Ezrah jumped as it opened up, and he nearly fell into bubbling lava. It was all around him, and he stood on a lone patch of stone. The stone was shrinking, eaten up by the boiling lava. The next stone was too far. He slid a foot forward, and a pebble tumbled into the lava, sizzling. Breaths came hard and fast, his heart pounding against his ribcage. If he didn't think of something soon, he'd be burned alive. Ezrah took deep breaths, controlling his rapid inhales and exhales.

Ezrah touched his spark. It was there.

Don't be afraid, Fera's voice echoed in his head.

She had gotten through this, so could he.

Magma continued to eat away at his dwindling island, and he had an idea. He put his hand to the stone and hummed, breathing his power in. Ezrah imagined the stone moving forward and pictured the threads. A spike of anger fueled him, thinking of Nalia, of Logan, of all those who tried to control and hurt. His anger gave sustenance to the spark in his mind, and thick brown and red filaments moved, parting the magma. It was simply hot stone and fire. His island moved like a rock skipping across water. He advanced towards the solid ledge in the distance. Each moment, his little island dwindled more. It rocked dangerously back and forth, sloshing about in the viscous magma. Ezrah cried out, nearly touching the hot lava. As his rock slowed, he risked it. He leapt with all his strength, pressing off. He landed, clipping the edge of solid ground and rolling. Breathing hard, sweat covering his body from heat and fear, he glanced back. His tiny little rock sunk into the magma bubbling and burning, then was gone. He sighed and wiped his hands, moving forward.

Fire and flame traps sprung at every turn. He dodged them until he was standing, staring at the next part of the maze. Walls on either side were craggy stone, the floor a soft earth.

The element of stone.

He could handle stone.

Stone was solid, unyielding, and stubborn. He had those qualities in abundance.

After a few turns, he stumbled upon a chamber of stone. Ahead, he saw a chasm descending into bottomless dark. Spanning the chasm were round pillars of stone, hundreds of them. It seemed like a trap.

Ezrah didn't like it. Fera wouldn't have fallen for that. Then how had Fera passed this? Then he saw… On the wall, a ledge like the lower lip of a giant had been extended. Fera must have created it. As he moved towards it, he realized it was now little more than a brittle ledge with gaps too big to cross. Chunks had been taken out of that walkway. Why? Ezrah stared at the ceiling that was dark. The magical maze sometimes showed the real roof, sometimes a low ceiling. Now it looked like a dome of stone. Was it real? It didn't matter.

He could try to do the same, to carve out a tunnel or make a ledge of stone. If he did, he'd exhaust his spark and have nothing left for the next trial. He needed to conserve his magic. He was already tired to his bones. Depleting one's spark felt like being drugged, his mind a tad fuzzy, his steps a little leaden. Yet, it wouldn't slow him. *Damn the trap*, he thought and leapt onto the first round pillar.

It had plenty of room, about four or five feet, enough to land and even roll. Each gap was of similar distance, wide enough that if he got a running start, he could do it. As his feet touched the stone, however, there was a rumbling.

A crack sounded from above, a huge stone whistled. He leapt to the next stone as earth and rubble showered about him. He looked back and saw a giant lance had pulverized the pillar where he'd stood moments ago.

He shot a bolt of sun upwards, illuminating the ceiling, and saw them. Thousands of stalactites, like stone spears. Landing on the pillars must have offset them. Sure enough, there was another rumble and a crack. Ezrah leapt. This time, without the running start, his foot slipped on the lip of the pillar, and he fell. He scrambled for purchase on the pillar's edge. His fingers slipped over the dusty stone, nearly tumbling. In the last moment, with a hint of stone, he turned the earth beneath his hands into putty, forming a lip of stone to hold onto, then solidified the stone once more. The handle was a perfect grip. A stray stalactite clipped him, cutting into his back. Snarling against the pain, he dragged himself back onto the pillar, standing tall once more.

He looked ahead and heard the groan and crack of stone above. He'd never make it at this pace. Two dozen pillars stood between him and a safe ledge in the distance.

He knew what he had to do. He had to run.

The talisman still glowed in his head, sensing his friend was near, alive, and afraid.

For Fera, Ezrah balled his hands into fists and sprinted with all his strength.

Another spear fell.

It smashed at his side, sending him almost off course.

Another exploded before him, shards spraying. He held up his arms, and the little rocks cut into his recently healed arm. Crying out in pain, Ezrah blinked away tears and pushed onward. More stone rained. The ledge in the distance seemed impossibly far. Fera's voice echoed in his head. *You are more than you think.* Doubt like a shadow crept over his mind. Another spear careened, and he stopped in the nick of time. Yet its spray of dust smashed into his eyes. He couldn't see. *Don't be afraid,* her voice whispered.

Fear overwhelmed him. How could he not be afraid? Any moment, a spear of stone could smash down, ending him, ending it all.

Then he breathed out, letting go, just a bit more than normal. The flame in his mind was hot and suddenly livid. The spark roared. He touched it, just for a brief moment. He cast thick threads. The world rumbled at his feet, more stone spraying, dust making him squint and cough. Fear returned, and the spark dwindled. He rose and ran forward. He felt a shadow following him. Above, a thick slab of stone hovered over him, suspended by his own magic. Instead of gawking, Ezrah marveled and ran. The slab reverberated with hammering blows. It took the brunt of the damage. *Please hold together,* he thought. A crack formed. Then another. It split down the center as more stalactites showered about Ezrah. *No! Hold on!* He forced his legs to leap, jumping from one to the next. Ahead, there was a landing before a corridor, an end to stone pillars. The slab of stone finally cracked completely, and Ezrah roared, shoving it ahead of him, using it as a ramp. Then he lifted his hands, threading more stone.

His slab shot up, if only for a moment. He pressed off it with his feet, and it shot him into the air. Ezrah soared. He was screaming, realizing only now, floating through the air, that he had no way of landing without shattering every bone. In the last minute, he pulled some more of his spark, like the last sip from a dwindling water skein, and softened the stone ahead to muck. He landed, his legs jolting

41

from the pain but not breaking, and he rolled through the muck and into the corridor. Huffing and puffing, he looked back, hearing the sudden silence.

Dust coated everything; clouds of it hung in the air. Through it, he saw his slab as it slid off a pillar and tumbled into the depths.

I did it… Seven hells, I did it!

He almost whooped in joy, but then he remembered Fera. The metal talisman glowed a bright orange in his mind again. Ezrah groaned, rising, his body battered. He brushed himself off feeling bruised from head to toe. *If I get through this, I'm going to sleep for a week.* He turned, facing his path ahead.

The corridor beyond was dark, and an eerie purple glow suffused the air.

"Moon," he whispered to himself. Notoriously one of the hardest elements to control, let alone master, and he grumbled, "Great." Then he shook himself and stepped into the shadows, speaking reassuringly into the darkness, "You've got this, Ez. You just mastered stone and fire. This'll be easy."

After a while of walking in shadows and nothing bad happening, Ezrah's unease grew. He should have felt a surge of confidence, however—all his life, he was used to bad things happening. He knew good things wouldn't last. Sure enough, the dark hall ended abruptly, and with Ezrah's next footfall, the shadows of the hall receded. He stepped into an otherworldly plane.

Swallowing, his every step slowed.

He was suddenly outside, or what felt like outside.

No, it was still The Great Maze.

The sky above showed brooding, roiling clouds as if thunder and lightning were moments away. Only it was silent. So perfectly silent, Ezrah could hear his own heartbeat thrumming in his ears. In the distance was a spindly leafless tree. Beyond that, a keep of shadows lit a menacing purple that bordered on black, like dark purple clouds. "What is that?" It reminded him of Narim, the shadowed Great Kingdom of Moon, only more sinister.

As Ezrah walked, his footsteps felt strange.

The ground had changed.

42

Beneath him was dark glass, and a mirrored surface reflected the storming sky.

Ezrah shook his head, trying to shut it out. *Focus, boy,* Calas's voice echoed in his head. He was right. None of it mattered. He just needed to find the corridor again, find the next part of the maze. In the distance, was only endless dark space. It felt as if the maze, all of it, had disappeared, and he'd been dumped in some strange alternate shadow world.

It was common for the element of moon. Moon was renowned for bending space and even time. At the highest levels of moon manipulation, or so it was said, one could step through a portal made of moon and land themselves on the other side of Farhaven. Only Dared, the Ronin of Moon, the fallen guardian, had such a skill. This place…it seemed like it was made of such oddities.

"Fera!" he shouted, and his voice was swallowed, muffled as if yelling into a pillow.

It gave him the shivers.

He took slow steps.

"Fera!" he called again. Silence. Ezrah growled. "Right, whatever creepy, foul thing is going to attack me, now's the time. Get it over, so I can save Fera."

As if on command, something gripped his ankle. Ezrah yelped, and his heart leapt into his throat as he jumped into the air. He sent a cascade of fire where he had just stood, searing and scorching. It careened off the dark glass, and he finally stopped, heaving heavy breaths. When the fire faded, there was no sign of his assailant. "Bloody creepy moon," he grumbled. Then something seemed to shift beneath the glass, like fish in a vat of oil, trapped beneath the frozen surface. Ezrah swallowed. *I can do this.* Hope. He embraced the power of sun, filling his hand with the element until it made his palm glow white, translucent.

Reaching out tentatively, he touched the black glass.

Beneath the glass was an abyss of swirling, inky liquid. It looked like churning clouds or perhaps dark water, but thicker and slower, like oil. He gulped, afraid the glass was going to break at any moment. He held his glowing hand there for a moment longer, searching for something. Then he saw it. A face. He almost stumbled back, but he forced himself to stay, keeping his hand pressed to the cool glass. Clinging to hope, he brightened the yellow orb of sun in his hand to see better. The face neared, resolving itself. It peered back at him, its features all too familiar. Wild, wavy brown hair, an oval face, and bright grey-green eyes. It was his own. Ezrah's blood turned to ice. Slowly, the face showed a body with the vague shape of flowing robes. A hand reached out as well, with a glowing purple orb. Moon. As if it was matching him, reflecting the opposite spell.

"You can't be real," Ezrah breathed.

The figure said nothing, only smiling, a sinister light in its eyes.

Ezrah stepped back. As he did, the mirrored version of himself stepped out of the glass to stand a foot away from him. Robes like his, only threadbare, wavered slowly as if still underwater. A perfect image of Ezrah, if more ominous in every way. A faint sheen of eerie purple surrounded his shadow self's body. "You're not real."

Its mouth moved, and a haunting voice like a whispered husk of his own followed, "You're not real."

Ezrah fists trembled at his side. "What are you?"

His shadow laughed and answered, "I am you. A shadow of you. A part of you that you wish to deny. The truest you. The fearful you, the powerful you."

A cry sounded far ahead.

Fera.

Cursing his shadow self, Ezrah turned, sprinting towards the purple keep. He had no idea where the corridor was, but he had to try somewhere. Maybe the keep was an illusion. Legs pumping, the dark version of himself reappeared, rising out of the glass in front of him once more, blocking his path. "You cannot run from yourself," his shadow taunted.

"Out of my way!" Ezrah snarled, sending a bolt of fire.

His shadow only smiled and lifted a hand, his inky robes undulating as it did. A purple portal of moon appeared from thin air and swallowed the fire. Another dark portal opened to Ezrah's right with a *vwoom*. His own fire shot out, and he barely lifted a hand to send out a flood of water. Water collided with fire, and a warm spray misted over him.

Ezrah growled, facing his shadow self. His blood was hot. "I don't have time for this!"

"Time?" his shadow replied, tilting its head in amusement. He unsheathed an obsidian blade with a sheen of purple. "There is no time in this place. No space. Moon bends these things to its will, just as I will bend you to mine!" With that, Ezrah's shadow attacked.

Ezrah dove out of the sword's path, landing painfully hard on his shoulder. As he did, he sent a blast of fire. The fire shot towards his shadow. This time, his shadow sliced it from the air, advancing.

Ezrah scrambled to his feet.

His shadow cut, and Ezrah reached up, threading the element of moon. The sword froze. He held the moon blade in place. Only Ezrah's command over the moon was weak, and the blade slowly descended. It scratched a bloody line in his forehead, burning, and Ezrah shrieked in pain. Unable to hold the sword any longer, Ezrah rolled to the side. The moon blade crashed into the dark mirror. Again, his shadow stalked forward. It slashed, stabbed, and shot orbs of moon. Ezrah could barely catch a breath, avoiding the onslaught. He tried to retaliate, though every time Ezrah shot a bolt of fire, a lance of ice, or threads of flesh, his shadow effortlessly dipped and ducked his magic.

As if his dark self knew all of his moves before he did.

"Embrace your despair," his shadow snarled.

"Never!"

"So be it." Dark Ezrah lifted the purple blade and stabbed it down.

The glass cracked beneath Ezrah, and he ran as it forked and fell away. The cracking ground was faster, and Ezrah fell into the dark liquid. Ezrah's mouth filled with the viscous fluid, and his legs, boots, and robes weighed him down. He spat and coughed. The liquid was warm and thick. Terrified, he tried to claw his way out, to keep his head above the dark liquid, but it was no use, and at last, a smile on his shadow's face, he was dragged down, into the dark waters.

He gasped a final breath before he was plunged into darkness.

Time slowed beneath the waters, and a strange purple light suffused everything. Ezrah clawed for the surface, but it was slipping away. Too far. The light and his shadow figure stood at the top of the hole where he had fallen, yet that, too, dwindled to a pinpoint. He was trapped beneath the darkness. His lungs burned. His mind was filled with horror. *I'm drowning! This…this can't be how it ends.* Terror made his mind a whirlpool, thoughts colliding and swirling, unable to think of anything but to claw to the surface. It wasn't working.

Sun! I need sun!

However, hope was required to thread the element of sun, and hope was small, an idea too far away for Ezrah to grasp. Suddenly, Ezrah touched something. He kicked and squirmed in terror. Out of instinct, he summoned a dark purple glow and touched it. The glow lit the object, and he saw it was a corpse, a fallen warrior from another age. The dead warrior still clung to a sword as it hovered in the purple liquid. A ray of the dark light lit the corpse's face. At that moment, time froze... Ezrah's racing mind slowed. The warrior's expression was cast in fear. Just like Ezrah. As if up until his last moments, he had been afraid.

His shadow self's words echoed in his mind: *Embrace your despair.* Suddenly, Ezrah understood.

46

He couldn't run from his fear. All his life, he had. Instead, he needed to accept it, breathe it in, then let it go. Only by accepting and embracing it could he leave it behind. So Ezrah let the feeling fill him, all that he had been denying, fearing, and running from. Fear of his weakness, of Fera's demise, of not being enough, of being small, abandoned on the street, dust filling his nose, kicked into some alley and forgotten.

As soon as he did, he felt power.

He let out a bubble of air, some of his last breath, and tracked it as it rose upward, pointing his direction out. Hope filled him. Following that trajectory, he sent a ray of sun shooting ahead, lighting his path and the way to the surface. At the same time, Ezrah pried the sword from the dead warrior's grip. Then he swam and kicked with all his might. He burst free of the dark waters, landing on the mirrored glass.

The viscous water sluiced from his form as he snarled and eyed his dark self. "I know what you are now." He glowed with sun, his hands translucent. "You are nothing but my own fear." As Ezrah embraced his fear, he breathed in.

As he did, cracks of light appeared on his shadow's body.

The cracks spread, and his shadow self watched, snarling. The eerie copy of himself suddenly lunged, crying out in a final attack with sword arcing down.

Ezrah wanted to flinch beneath the sword's attack, only he didn't shift, didn't move. Instead, he voiced from the depths of his heart, "I'm not afraid of you anymore."

With those words, his shadow burst into a thousand glass shards of black. These too were dissolved by light, and Ezrah felt his spirit and the shadow self merge as one. A sense of peace came over him. He turned and raced onward towards the dark keep in the distance. With his next step, the world and the realm of shadows dissolved. He was standing in the corridor.

Ezrah had a sinking suspicion that not much time had passed—as if the battle with his shadow self had taken only a fraction of time. He remembered his shadow's words. *Moon distorts space and time.*

A sharp, desperate cry sounded.

Fera!

Ezrah dashed onward, following the talisman's pull, and turned the next corridor, only to find himself surrounded by a hallway of vines and roots. The element of leaf. Wrist-thick vines snapped out. One grabbed his arm, and another circled his ankle. Ezrah hacked and cut them with the dead warrior's sword.

More shot out, around his arms, legs, and neck, dragging Ezrah to the ground.

However, his anger was stronger.

Fire drew on the rage in his heart, and his spark listened more easily than ever.

Orange threads swirled about his body, from his feet to his head, and he snapped his fingers. Fire roared, coursing over his body, encasing him in a living shield of flames. Root, vine, every living thing shrieked, burning and shriveling, retreating. His bonds broken, Ezrah rose and kept moving when he felt the talisman's glow.

It burned in his mind, so close.

Not ahead but beneath him.

Ezrah stared down and saw a bulbous growth of green, like a giant knot from a tree. A muffled cry sounded inside the writhing mass of vines. Anger flared, and Ezrah's hand blazed. He reached to touch the vines, then froze.

Fera was encased in them. He couldn't risk hurting her, especially not with his spark surging as it was. He drew on the element of leaf.

47

Leaf, or nature, was all about life, protecting it, nurturing it, and being one with your surroundings. He needed little encouragement. Filaments of green slammed into the growth.

Immediately, the knot of vine and roots unwound itself. He fed more until he saw her face. Fera… Her skin was ashen. A thick root was wrapped around her neck. Ezrah grabbed it, sending threads of green out of the root, draining its spark. It shriveled to a husk, and he tossed it aside, then dragged Fera out as carefully as he could. She was still, too still. Dread filled him to his core. Ezrah put his ear to her chest, feeling a faint rise and fall and soft, warm breath on his cheek.

She was alive, but barely.

He pressed his hands onto her heart, threading flesh.

Bruises vanished on her neck and arms. The cracked rib fused itself, and she seemed to breathe easier. Ezrah heaved a sigh. At the same time, he felt drained. "That's the best I can do for now. It'll have to do until we find a real Reaver." He looked about. This deep in the maze, he knew the only way was forward. *If we can reach the end, there has to be a way out. The madness has to end. After all, Nalia had survived it.* Nalia. This sent worried thoughts of Calas, but Ezrah shoved them down and spoke, "We have to keep moving." Ezrah picked up Fera, putting her on his back like a log across his shoulders. It was the only way to carry someone bigger for a long time. Calas had taught him the technique. Using vines, he tied her to his back to ensure she'd stay secure. When had using leaf become so easy? The most he'd ever done until now was grow a seed into a sprout. Things were becoming easier inside the maze. As if under duress, something was burgeoning inside of him.

As he walked, Ezrah's legs felt strong.

"I'm glad you're light," he told her. Again, it made little sense. Ezrah wasn't tall or strong for his age. When other fourteen-year-old boys were filling out, muscle packing onto bone, Ezrah's arms were thin. However, now Fera *was* light over his shoulders. Perhaps he was just delirious from exhaustion, and he'd collapse any moment. Either way, Calas's wisdom again echoed in his ears, '*When all the problems of the world seem to be mounting against you, focus only on what you can do. Focus on moving forward.*' So Ezrah plodded on, feeling oddly invigorated.

48

"We can do this," he said encouragingly to Fera. "I'm not sure how I got through moon or how you did. I nearly died to that shadow thing, and that stone ledge of yours? That was genius. Still, we've come this far." He counted in his head. *Fire, stone, moon, and leaf.* Four down. "Only five more to go. Easy." Ezrah chuckled nervously, trying to sound brave. As he moved through the jungle of leaf and vine, watching his surroundings, eyes flickering at every little shift, he continued to talk to Fera to distract himself. "You know, you're really going to owe me when this is all over."

Fera was silent, her breathing soft now.

Walking faster, he tried not to think about how limp she felt. Luckily, vines seemed just as afraid of him, recoiling when he drew near. "However, I might owe you a *small* apology. Don't be mad, but I kind of… maybe sort of…promised Aiden a date with you."

Fera was silent.

He sighed as if relieved, wiping his brow dramatically. "Ah, good, I'm glad you're not upset. You know this might be the longest we've ever talked without you calling me a fool. I'm sure you'll make up for it, though, when you're awake." Ezrah kept talking to Fera just to keep his thoughts off their surroundings. Vines slithered about his feet like snakes. Fera was his handhold on reality when he felt like he was losing his mind in this twisted labyrinth. After a while of jabbering, he confessed, "Really, I am sorry about Aiden. I know how much of a fan you are of him." She hated Aiden. Or was it Caiden? It was likely both. Fera didn't get along with many people. Just Ezrah.

He'd always wondered why.

Ezrah stepped over a root that reached for his ankle, and it shriveled back from a burst of green. Fera was the prodigy. When all the world looked up to her, feared her, or respected her, she only seemed to care about him. He'd never felt so special, and at the same time, so unworthy. He whispered aloud, asking her again, "Why me?"

With his next step, the walls turned red.

"Seven hells of Remwar," he cursed, freezing in place. He sighed. *Flesh. Great.* His least favorite element. "Why does it have to be flesh?" He looked at Fera hanging over his shoulder. She looked peaceful, eyes closed. "If only you were awake. This is your specialty, not mine." He

49

shook himself. *No, I've got this. I only have to get to the center. Then there has to be salvation.*

Determined, he continued on.

A fog fell over the maze, and his steps began to slow as he waded into a thin pool of standing water. He took a step, and his foot hit something. He used some of his remaining spark to clear away the fog and saw…it wasn't water he was standing in but a pool of blood. Burning away more mist revealed walls made of bone. Femurs, skulls, finger bones. It was a skeletal bulwark. Bones floated in the pool of blood. That's what he'd kicked. "Bloody great," he growled.

He looked back.

Calas, you better be alright. With luck, the Devari blademaster had beaten Nalia. Ezrah looked ahead, pushing onward. Fear and doubt wormed their way in as Ezrah continued to wade his way through the blood. Suddenly, he felt a shift in the air. Another element.

50   Using the element of flesh, he sensed an object of bone slicing towards him.

Sucking in a breath, Ezrah ducked.

Crash.

The huge axe cleaved through the air, smashing into the wall of bones and sending shards of white flying. A moment slower, Ezrah would have lost his head. He backpedaled, banishing some of the fog ahead.

Out of the white vapor stepped a huge creature. With a head like a bull and the torso and arms of a heavily muscled man, he knew what it was. A minotaur. A thing of myth and legend. Most horrifying was its skin, or lack thereof. As if victim of a horrifying experiment, it had no skin, exposing red muscle and white tendon. Armor covered parts of the beast's body, shoulders, chest, and groin. It had a faint red sheen to it, along with its horns. Bloodstone. In its heavy grip was a huge white axe made from bone, as if carved from an ancient gargantuan creature.

This isn't real, Ezrah thought, breath quickening, backing up. "You can't be real…"

The minotaur snorted a hot breath through its wide nostrils pierced by a thick metal ring.

The beast took a step forward on bent legs, advancing.

"Wait, hold on, can't we just talk about this?" Snarling, it raised its great axe made of bone. "Bloody hells." Ezrah threaded, feeling again oddly alive as if the maze was sending him power. He delved into his body. All he felt was rage and protection. With no vines nearby, aside from the ones keeping Fera slung tightly across his shoulders, he resorted to his old ally and sent out a torrent of fire, then more fire, hoping to burn the thing to a crisp. He cried out, pouring enough so that the blood bubbled and boiled before him, and the bone walls turned black. At last, he let the fire die. Smoke cleared, and the minotaur stepped out of the smoke. Its armor glowed, as well as its huge curled horns, shining a vibrant red.

No... He hadn't even touched the creature. How the hell was he supposed to kill a beast that he couldn't touch with the spark?

Again, the minotaur snorted and heaved the big axe and slammed it down, splashing, creating a wave of blood. The creature was surprisingly quick.

Ezrah barely had time to jump aside. With Fera on his back, tied by the vines, his leap became a stumble, and he awkwardly tumbled into the pool of blood. Coughing and gagging on the thick metallic taste of blood, Ezrah pushed himself to his hands and knees, hearing and seeing cloven hooves sloshing through the river of blood.

The creature was huge, looming over him, nearing.

Fear rooted him.

Move, Ezrah, move!

A hoof smashed into his belly. The vines snapped on his back, and he was sent splashing in the blood, rolling away from Fera. Pain blotted his vision, and he lifted his head above the blood just a moment to gasp a breath. The blow felt as if it'd cracked every rib in his stomach. He could scarcely breathe, and his vision was blurred by blood and tears as the creature advanced, making growling bellows. Somewhere, he knew Fera was beneath the blood, drowning. It was all happening too quickly. This wasn't meant for him. *I'm not supposed to be here. This is an accident.* His rage fell away to fear, and Ezrah scrambled back. "Please..."

Don't be afraid, Ez.

He'd always been afraid.

He was lost in a sudden memory.

51

* * *

They were burning everything. The world smelled like smoke, and Ezrah was about to die. The gaunt-faced man raised the dagger, ready to stab. To gut him where he lay, frozen in the sand. Ezrah sniffled, tears running down his face. Run! Ezrah told himself. Only there was nothing but fear. All-consuming fear.

The thief snorted, "Can't even run, can you? Fear's got you? You're going to piss yourself before you die." The thief's dagger fell.

"Wait!" Anna shrieked, pulling herself up, looking dazed. Her dress was half-ripped, her face soot-stained and bloody. The bony thief paused as if amused. "Please," she cried out, "don't touch the boy. He's lost enough for any one lifetime. His parents, his sisters. I'm all he has. Do what you will to me, but leave the boy. I beg of you."

The boney thief chuckled, then turned on Anna. "What bravery. Let's see how brave you are." He advanced on her.

Ezrah's heart hammered until he thought it would burst through his body.

He was paralyzed.

Why? Why wasn't he stronger? If only he was stronger…

* * *

Suddenly, he was tossed back into the moment.

The minotaur loomed over him, and the axe head fell.

Caught in that same fear, Ezrah couldn't move. Just like then, his dread was too all-consuming.

At the last moment, he saw something in the corner of his eye. Fera. She was standing on her feet. Wavering, looking half-dead. Thin threads of flesh, bits of tan and red, extended from her hand. A finger-thick bone jettisoned through the air, smashing through the creature's abdomen, spurting blood. The minotaur roared in pain, and the bone axe veered off course, skimming over Ezrah's skull. Still, his hands were extended before him, trying to shield what he knew was coming. He couldn't pull away in time as the axe carved, severing his fingers on his right hand. Pain erupted, terrible and sudden, then nothing. Staring at his mutilated hand, now adding to the pool of blood.

Shock took his pain away.

Anger replaced it. The beast pulled the sharpened bone from its chest with one hand, then gripped the huge axe in both, and swung again. Ezrah ducked the next strike, grabbed something in the bloody water, and smashed it into the creature's fleshy leg. He realized it was a jagged piece of bone. The creature snarled, grabbed him, and tossed him against the wall. Ezrah hit his head, and the world swam. Ears ringing, the minotaur advanced again, splashing towards him.

"Fight me, you stupid mountain of muscle!" Fera taunted and sent shard after shard of bone. Some broke against the creature's armor while others pierced its flesh. Finally, it turned, letting out a growl, throaty and deep, charging at her.

Fera's legs buckled, exhausting the last of her energy.

Ezrah picked himself up, but he could only watch.

Just like last time.

No more.

He wasn't afraid of his weakness but of something else.

Memories tried to resurface, only for him to push them down. Still, seeing the beast advance for Fera, he relinquished some of his fear and gave in. Letting go, Ezrah gave into the spark inside of him, admitting his power. The spark, like tinder, caught flame.

Threads as thick as a man's leg flew through the air, and the bloodstone armor on the minotaur's back grew red. The minotaur swung its axe, and it aimed towards Fera's head as she knelt in the pool of blood. Ezrah's power wasn't enough. The magic of the bloodstone armor was soaking it all up. So he poured more and more still, shouting at the top of his lungs as the axe descended. He was too slow. *More.* Tan and red filaments like glowing cords slammed into the beast's back as he demanded more power still.

Suddenly, he heard screams in his head.

Visions flashed before his eyes; memories of the whole town on fire, of walls leveled, of everything laid to waste. Immediately, like pulling hard on the reins of a horse about to gallop, he snuffed his power.

Opening his eyes, he saw it had been enough.

The gems inside the minotaur's armor had shattered, and the armor lost its glow. The pink and tan threads of flesh had done their work,

53

and he was inside the creature's mind. The axe stopped just before Fera's face. Ezrah breathed a tremulous breath.

Ezrah smiled wanly and lowered his hands. "Relax for a bit, will you?" he told the beast. "No more trying to kill us, if you please."

The minotaur let out a throaty growl and sank to its knees, bowing its head in subservience.

Fera's jaw hung, eyeing him and the minotaur.

He neared her, stumbling. Fera rushed to his side, but he caught himself. "I'm... I'm all right," Ezrah insisted.

"You damn fool."

"I'm fine, really."

"Your hand."

Ezrah lifted his palm and eyed his fingers, trying to slow his breaths. He felt the severed digits sitting in the pool of blood. He lifted them out of the bloody waters into the air. Slowly, they floated over his bleeding hand. "Let's hope this works..." With thin threads of flesh, like a surgeon's sutures, he tied the nerves, muscle, and skin back together, knitting them until...his hand was whole once more. Scared they would fall off, he flexed his fingers, testing them gently. "Still hurts. Feels like they're still missing, but guess that'll have to do."

Fera's jaw was hanging. "Have to do? Ezrah, you were missing fingers."

He shrugged. "Now I'm not."

"Where in the seven hells did you learn to do that?"

He touched her chin, closing her hanging jaw. "Read it in a book. Fingers can be reattached as long as the time between severing wasn't too long, and the flesh and nerves are still intact."

She lifted a brow.

"What? I *can* read."

"Right..." Fera said slowly and eyed the minotaur. It knelt in the blood, its red muscled chest rising and falling with heavy breaths, head bowed. Bone still protruded from its body on its leg where Ezrah had stabbed it, and blood leaked from its chest wound. It was a mess, though it didn't seem to hinder the creature. Most importantly, it was subdued. "And this? Did you really just control a minotaur—a mythical being? When you couldn't control a mouse?"

54

"Not so mythical," he said with a small laugh, then grew serious. "I… I heard your voice. You told me not to be afraid anymore. Still working on it."

"You're starting to see," she said with a smile.

What do we do now? He wondered, looking at the blood waters, the pacified minotaur, and the thick walls of bone. What would Calas do? "C'mon," Ezrah told her gruffly, trying to sound like his unwavering mentor, "we can't stay here. I can carry you again."

She sniffed, crossing her arms. "I'm not some hapless maiden needing rescue." Then she looked ahead at the corridor, seeing it turn from white bone and blood to the gray luster of metal.

Ezrah rose, following her gaze.

He knew what she was thinking.

Metal, water, sun, and wind were still ahead. It was a daunting thought that sucked the wind from Ezrah's sails. He was so tired. He couldn't keep going like this. What awaited them next? Afterall, Flesh was supposedly the weakest of the nine elements. He could only imagine the peril of sun, water, and metal, let alone wind. Wind, an element only a Ronin could conjure.

Fera swallowed but grabbed his wrist. "C'mon, Ez…the only way is forward."

Ezrah turned to the walls of bones. "Actually, I've a better idea." He eyed the kneeling minotaur.

Fera shook her head. "We have to continue. The rules of this place will keep pushing us back towards the finish line."

A smirk grew on his face. "What are rules if they're not meant to be broken?" Sure, the maze wanted them to continue trial after trial, but when was he ever one to follow the rules? He remembered Titan and the bread. "Let's try this my way."

He flicked a hand, and the minotaur strained, turning to face the wall.

The wall didn't glow red with bloodstone.

Then if the wall was reinforced, it was likely with magic.

Magic.

Calas's words returned to him. *Anything and everything has a flaw. You just have to find its weak point.*

Ezrah grinned, raising his hands, sending more flesh threads. Like a puppet, the minotaur rose from its kneeling position, and cast aside

55

its axe. The beast snorted. Ezrah flung his hands, and the minotaur charged. Its horns glowed, and it smashed into the wall. Bone erupted in chunks. As it did, he saw a barrier that looked like a web of clear glass. Each time the minotaur smashed its horns into it, the glass sent out tremors. Again, he commanded the beast. Suddenly, he saw a crack in the magical glass. Ezrah sent more. Finally, bone and glass burst, and the minotaur charged through the cloud of dust.

He looked at Fera and gave a bow, gesturing, "After you, my lady."

Fera, her eyes wide, walked through the mist.

Ezrah followed.

Beyond, the minotaur waited inside a giant dome, its horns glowing red. In the center was an altar containing the Star of Magha, showing all nine points. "You never cease to surprise," Fera whispered, looking about, and then pointed, "What...what is that?"

At the heart of the altar, sitting on a pedestal carved with strange runes, an orb waited. Radiant light issued from it. Blue, green, red, yellow, orange, purple, brown, white, and black. It swirled with all the colors of the elements, held behind a crackling cage of power. Ezrah reached out.

"Ez! What are you doing?"

"There's something about it. I feel pulled towards it."

"So do moths before a flame and mice to cheese before the trap falls. Don't touch it. It can't be safe." Ezrah felt his newly healed fingers grow warm. The golden cage of light was hot as if it would sear the flesh from his bones. Still, Ezrah felt compelled to take another step. Fera shouted, "Dammit, Ez! Do you ever listen to anything anyone says?"

The cage that guarded the orb, as if sensing his presence, disappeared.

He looked to Fera.

She swallowed. "Don't look at me. I've no idea what's happening right now. Well, go on, touch it. You've come this far and clearly know more than I do."

His palms felt clammy, and he shook his head. "Not without you." He reached out for her.

Fera took a deep breath, then nervously, she stepped up to his side and took his hand.

"Together," he said.

As one, they reached out, their hands moving to the orb at the same time. The elements glowed brighter and brighter as if wanting to burst free. Right before touching it, however, Ezrah felt the ground cracking beneath his feet, and he stumbled, falling and losing his grip on Fera.

"What's happening?" Fera called as the altar continued to rumble and shake.

Where the altar fractured, white light bloomed.

"I don't know! Grab my hand!" Ezrah shouted and lunged, though again, the ground rumbled, and he fell, tumbling, missing her grip. "No, Fera!" She fell away from him, crying out, and his vision was taken by a rainbow of colors assaulting his vision. Blue, green, red, yellow, orange, purple, brown, black, and white. He continued to plummet, his stomach going up into his throat. Then it was over.

Silence.

Opening his eyes, Ezrah blinked and saw his surroundings.

Perfect emptiness resembling a white void.

Dazed, he rose to his feet. "Where in the seven hells… What is this?" Then he called out, "Anyone? Fera?" His voice echoed in a chamber of nothing, then fell away as if it was receding into a great distance.

From above, a figure appeared, floating down on a mote of glowing golden dust. Ezrah's skin tingled in awe. His mouth was gaping, and he shut it. His mind spun, trying to comprehend what he was seeing. The figure's outline could be faintly seen, and nine elements, glowing spheres, slowly rotated around its body. Like its voice, it was both masculine and feminine. "Welcome, my child."

Ezrah shielded his eyes, stepping back, as the figure came to a rest a dozen paces away. "Who…who are you? And what is this place? Am I dreaming?"

"Not dreaming, finally awake."

"Then where am I?"

"You are in an Altar of Truth. Built by myself and my two firstborn. It is a place to test those who are worthy."

"Right," he said slowly, as if that made sense, then squinted. He pulled away his arm, trying to stare into the light, but it hurt his eyes. "Worthy of what? Where's Fera? She better be safe."

An arm pointed out of the bright light, pointing down. "See for yourself."

Ezrah stared down at his feet and saw that it fell away, and the maze was beneath him. Then he saw her, standing where he had left her, on the center of the altar. She was still frozen in time, stuck in a world of white like his. Now he saw that the vision of it crumbling had all been in his mind. Somewhere was Nalia and Calas—only he couldn't see anything clearly from this height. Only the flare of magic from each of the points of the star, though slowly the bright colors dimmed, the maze's magic dying. Reaching the center must have ended the maze's traps.

"Satisfied?" the figure of light asked. Ezrah could still sense its amusement.

"A little," he said, crossing his arms stubbornly. "You still didn't answer... Who are you?"

58   The figure's light pulsed. "I am simply one who wishes to pull back the veil, to show the potential of men and women. You are more than you could ever imagine."

Something inside him thrummed as if he knew the answer the figure was avoiding, though he was afraid of it. Again he swallowed, looking about the space of white. "I don't understand. Why am I here? I thought this was a test of Reavers to attain one's fourth stripe."

"Lies from those who wish to rule the world. That is almost true, but not quite."

"What do you mean? What is the truth?"

"It's a test I created to find the next mortal who could balance the eight elements, to understand their different purposes—moon for cunning, flesh for heart, leaf for nurturing, water for surrender, fire for passion, stone for tenacity, though I'll admit, you might possess the last one in excess."

"This isn't right. I didn't even complete it! What about sun?"

"Sun, you showed me the truth when you broke open the water barrels and gave the people of the desert who were dying of thirst a chance at life. That hope was your first test."

"You saw that? Still..." He shook his head. "What about metal? Water?"

"Metal you passed when you broke the plates on my minotaur's armor. Bloodstone is a gem, the purest form of what comprises metal. You didn't overload the gem as you thought; you shattered it from the inside. A feat not many can achieve."

Ezrah ran a hand through his hair. "That still leaves water."

Again, as if he was a Devari, Ezrah felt the figure of light's emotion. Mirth. "In the lake of moon, you were drowning, pulled down by the weight of your robes and shoes, enough to drag down any man. With a sword in your hand, you swam like a fish and even catapulted out of the waters." Again, that hidden smile. "Did you think you were simply a good swimmer?"

Ezrah snorted, feeling somehow embarrassed *and* proud. "Right, so you've got a lot of answers, but you still haven't answered the most important one. What's the point of it all? Why the test?"

"That's the easiest answer yet. To find someone who could help me guide the world towards truth and peace."

Truth and peace… Ezrah's jaw dropped. Arbiters were often called the guardians of truth and peace. "You mean…" Ezrah felt a shiver trace his whole spine. If this was really his body, it felt cold with a flush of sweat.

"An Arbiter," the figure of light answered. "You are that answer."

"You can't be serious. What about Nalia and the others who passed?"

"Another lie. Only one other has passed before you."

One other… The Patriarch. "You're saying I'm…"

"Not yet. An Arbiter is only born once they conjure a Grand Creation. An artifact that transforms the world, a creation summoned from the depths of the threader's soul. Though it requires enough power to make the world quake. I will teach you to tap into it. You are worthy of that power." The figure lifted a hand, and the pedestal rose with the orb, a perfect sphere of some rare material, clear with a diamond sheen. Inside were eight balls of flowing energy, making the sphere pulse with radiant colors. It was all of the elements flowing together, except for white. The whole of it made Ezrah's heart thrum, his pulse race, and he yearned to touch it. *Pure power.* "Grab the orb and pull the power of the eight elements into your soul."

Again, Ezrah stared at Fera, who stood on the altar, caught in her own ephemeral dream. "Both of you are special. There is a reason

59

why you've felt bound to one another all your lives. When it is time, she will follow," said the figure in a calm voice. "For now, it is yours."

Ezrah hesitated. The orb sat before him, drawing him. Slowly, he reached out. Power. Images flashed in his mind, searing his vision. Hills, buildings, all of it a wasteland. He shook his head, ripping his hand away and falling to his knees, crying. "I... I can't... I can't do it. I don't deserve this."

"That day is not your fault, Ezrah."

Looking down, Ezrah stared at his trembling hands, seeing blood that wasn't there. "I don't want that kind of power. Not ever again."

Sorrow resonated from the figure of light. "Sometimes, Ezrah, the power to do right requires the same power that can also do wrong."

Ezrah thought of Titan, of the gaunt-faced man beating Anna, cries filling his ears. All those who abused their power, and he was no exception. How was he to be any different? He shook his head, tears falling. "I...can't..."

A warm hand touched his shoulder, and a radiant light and warmth filled Ezrah. The figure answered solemnly, "Force is not the way of this test. Perhaps you are not ready."

The figure of light slowly began to fade, along with the chamber of white.

"I'm sorry," Ezrah called out as the white void disappeared.

Suddenly, he was back in the world, standing on the altar and holding the orb. Somehow it was placed in his hand, but he felt nothing from it. No radiating power. The maze around them still remained. It slowly dimmed, though flames still danced along the walls of the cavern. Fera was at his side, and as the white void vanished, her body slumped as if her strings were cut.

Ezrah scooped her up with one arm. "Fera!"

She regained her balance and looked about, perplexed. "What happened?" She put a hand to her head. "One moment we were reaching for the orb, for that—" she nodded to the glass sphere, "and the next, everything started crumbling. Then...you're here. Did you see anything? What'd I miss?"

"Nothing, just a bit of magic," he lied.

"Just a bit of magic? Ez, you're holding an orb of immeasurable power."

He shrugged. "Guess it must be broken."

She eyed him doubtfully. "Broken? Did you hit your head? Did I hit my head? Seven hells, did we both hit our heads?"

"Maybe," he said and looked down. The orb… It still churned with its multitude of colors, but it no longer filled him with any sort of feeling. As if it was just ornamentation. Ezrah understood. He had lost his chance to access the power the figure had offered him. *I won't become a monster*, he thought. "I made the right choice."

"What choice?" Fera asked.

"Nothing." He gave a grin. "Just talking to myself. Are you alright? Are you hurt?"

"Alright?" she asked, as if unsure how to answer. "Aside from being cast into a magical whirlpool of light that turned out to be my imagination, and just before that, nearly killed by a flesh minotaur and a dozen other obstacles in a maze of death?"

"Right, aside from that."

"Then I suppose I'm just fine. Though I've no idea how Nalia made it through that deathtrap in one piece."

"Maybe she didn't," Ezrah answered. At her questioning look, he coughed, looking to the maze.

She eyed it as well, both of them facing it. "Do you think anyone in the Citadel is going to believe us?"

He chuckled. "They never believed me before."

"I suppose not. Ezrah…" Tears began to fall down her face. "I never would have made it without you." She gripped him tightly, fingers digging into his cloak, just like she had before.

He pulled away. "Can you walk? We can't stay here. I swore I'd go back for Calas."

She nodded.

"What are you going to do with that?" She pointed to the minotaur that still stood at the broken entry of bone. "Keep it as a pet? More importantly, how do we get out of here? Please don't tell me the way we came."

"The maze is silent now," he said, looking around for a quicker path when something roared.

Fera cried out, "Ez, watch out!"

Ezrah turned barely in time to see a wall of flames advancing. Fera leapt before him, flinging her hands, and a shield of water formed. The fire turned to a cloud of steam. Fera wavered on her feet, and Ezrah grabbed her, keeping her up. At the same time, walking through the haze, Ezrah spotted a scarlet hem with four stripes.

"Nalia," Ezrah growled, cursing.

Power filled him.

Nalia swiped a hand, and the mist evaporated. She looked worse for wear with cuts and scrapes, her robes tattered and sliced at places. *Calas*, Ezrah knew. Nalia had a mottled green and purple bruise on her neck, and her red hair was wild. As if a spell had fallen from her, her beauty was shed now, like a mask thrown aside. Accentuated by the shadows from the flames all about, her sharp features were more haunting, more skeletal.

Ezrah looked about. Where was Calas? Wiping the blood from the corner of her mouth, Nalia staggered forth. "Look at you, my dear children. What a surprise you two turned out to be. Somehow, I always knew there was something special about you two. It was clever, using the minotaur's bloodstone horns to break through the maze." She reached out a hand. "Sadly, now the game is over. Kindly hand over the orb, and I might show you mercy."

"Ez, don't," Fera said, shaking her head, looking at him.

Ezrah pulled it back, holding onto it tighter. *Mercy.* He knew she was a liar.

Nalia tsked. "You make it sound like he has a choice, girl. Come, Ezrah, don't make this difficult."

"If you're so powerful, why didn't you risk the maze?" Ezrah asked.

She laughed haughtily. "Risk my life by entering this deathtrap? I let others do that for me."

Ezrah's blood ran cold.

Fera must have understood too. "How many, you mad witch? How many innocents have you lured here?"

"Ah, now you're catching on. Where did you think those talented Neophytes and Reavers mysteriously disappeared to over the years? They all turned out to be weak and useless pawns. Finally, I found a lamb strong enough to survive the maze and bring me the object of my desire."

"Where's Calas?" Ezrah demanded at last.

"Oh, that one. He was quite the nuisance. Took a while to put him down."

"No!" Ezrah screamed, sending angry fire.

A purple sphere appeared as Nalia threaded a portal of moon, redirecting his fire. Another portal opened up beside Ezrah, and fire burst forth. A tenacious fiber rose inside of him. He lifted a hand, breaking off a huge hunk of stone from the altar, raising it. The stone blocked the flame. Heaving ragged breaths, he threw the hunk. Nalia caught it in midair with thick threads of stone. She clenched her hand as if crumpling a paper. The rock disintegrated into dust. "I see you've gained some skills."

"Your little tricks won't work on me twice," Ezrah said and felt orange essence streaming off his body, his spark loud in his mind. "I'm not afraid of you."

"So it seems. Is the orb feeding you that power? I can only imagine what it will do in the hands of an experienced threader." Her eyes widened, hungry. "Give it to me."

"Never!"

Beside him, Fera sent thick threads of flesh.

Nalia flicked her gaze, looking bored. She burned the threads with fire then sent thicker threads of flesh to entangle Fera, pressing her to the ground. "Come, girl, you are nothing compared to me."

Ezrah lifted a hand.

Nalia sent more threads of flesh. The threads sank into his muscles like fangs. He tried to banish them. Nalia screamed, sending more. Just then, a figure appeared, leaping from the wall and cutting the threads holding Ezrah.

"Calas!"

The Devari stood like an enduring mountain. Calas's chainmail sleeve hung loosely, and his black and tan leather suffered a few scorches. Otherwise, he seemed unharmed as his sword glowed red. Ezrah felt a swell of hope. "It's alright, lad. I'm here now."

Ezrah choked back tears. "I…"

"I worried you, didn't I?"

"Maybe a little," he admitted with a small, choked laugh.

Calas snorted. "You didn't think I'd be that easy to take down, did you?" Then he eyed the elemental orb in Ezrah's hands. "That's what she's after, I'm guessing?"

He nodded. Suddenly, as it sat cradled in his hands, the orb warmed and shrank. It went from the size of his head to no bigger than an apple. Ezrah slipped it into his pocket. "Whatever we do, we can't let her get it."

"Got it." Calas raised his sword, pointing it at Nalia, who was fuming.

Fera rose, joining them. "Let's end this then, together."

They stood in a line facing their threat.

Nalia cackled, eyes wild. "You all have no idea, do you? You are still *nothing* compared to me. Come then, little mice. Come and face your end." She screamed a shrill cry, and sudden threads of flesh shot out. Ezrah tried to dissolve them, but they were too fast. Calas cut them again, sword glowing. It was a distraction. Nalia sent rocks and sharp bones flying towards them. Fera shouted, trying to catch all of the flying debris with threads. A rock grazed her, knocking her down. Ezrah called out to her, seeing her forehead bleeding from a gash. He turned, and the power within him swelled. Shouting, he sent an onslaught of fire and ice. Nalia flicked a hand. The threads dissolved, and she swept them aside.

Calas leapt, slashing.

She sent a rock veering towards them.

Ezrah could barely thread in time. It was all too much. He sent out thin, frayed threads of stone. It sent the rock hurtling towards Calas off course, just slightly. It missed his friend and hit Ezrah in the shoulder. Pain exploded. Ezrah staggered back, falling to his knees. Nalia unleashed a deluge of fire. It funneled into Calas's Devari blade. Inundated by flames, Calas was unable to press forward.

"Give me the orb, boy!" Nalia shouted. She flung a hand. Threads of flesh sunk into Ezrah. Against his will, Ezrah rose, and stumbled towards her, pulling the orb from his pocket. Her eyes grew hungry. "Give it to me, and I will have the power to rival Renalin himself."

Fera staggered to her feet, but threads of flesh slammed into her, holding her down. "Ezrah, don't!"

"I can't stop!" he shouted, nearing Nalia.

"Then take in the power of the orb as your own!" Calas shouted as fire assaulted him.

Ezrah breathed in, frantically trying to embrace the power of the elemental orb. Nothing happened. "I don't know how!"

Nalia's sneer deepened. "That's because you're not worthy."

He had been a fool to deny the power. Now it was too late. He'd lost his chance. Still, there had to be something he could do. If he couldn't take in the power, no matter what, he couldn't let Nalia have it. With the power of the orb in her hand, there'd be nothing to stop her. So with his next step, he roared, rebelling against every thread in his body, letting muscle and tissue tear. Ezrah threw the orb to the ground.

Nalia screamed, but she was too slow.

The orb shattered on the stone.

"You fool! Do you know what you've just done?" She shook with rage. "You just destroyed the power of a god!" Her eyes burned, twin flames. "I will make you pay for that. You will suffer." She raised her arms as dozens of threads of blue, orange, brown, gray, and more formed at her fingertips.

65

Calas roared, jumping through flames that held him back, being burned in the process. He cut, severing Nalia's outstretched hand, and her spell died. Blood poured, and she screamed, falling and clutching her bleeding stump.

Calas, smoke still rising from his scorched body, raised his sword to finish it, standing over the woman. "It's over."

Nalia's eyes were wide, and Ezrah saw a shifting of movement at her hip.

A dagger wiggling free of its sheath at her waist.

"Calas, watch out!" Ezrah shouted. He couldn't thread with Calas between him and Nalia. Nalia's dagger flew. Calas tried to parry, but the space between them was too narrow. Ezrah's heart caught in his throat. The ruby-hilted dagger embedded itself in Calas's chest. Calas's sword tumbled from his grip. Nalia rose and screamed, threading deep chords of flesh. Calas flew through the air, smashing into Ezrah, and they both rolled on the stone altar. Ezrah shook his head, clearing it. Fera lay nearby, unconscious.

Then he saw Calas.

His blood turned to ice as he scrambled to his friend's side.

Calas coughed blood, holding his wound. Seeing Ezrah, he gave a small smile. "I'm sorry, lad."

"Calas, no, please… I can't do this without you."

"You've always had the power in you. You know that as well as I." His eyes fluttered. He reached out his forearm.

Ezrah gripped it, tears flowing freely. "Please, no…"

"Sometimes, I forget you're only a boy, but I know you're going to change the world." Swallowing blood, Calas smiled, uttering, "Rekdala forhas." Ezrah knew those words. The old tongue, the code of the Devari, in greeting and departure. *With honor, until death.*

Then Calas closed his eyes and was gone.

He looked up to see Nalia approaching. She sighed. "He's dead, is he? Shame. He put up quite the fight. Goodbye, little oddity. You were a curious one, but in the end, strength is life, and weakness is death."

Ezrah's every muscle trembled with rage and sorrow as he knelt, hunched over Calas.

The orb was gone.

His spark flickered in his mind, wavering in and out like a candle on the edge of being snuffed by a strong breeze. Nalia's power grew, and she touched his head. Fire raged all around, burning and searing. Fera lay unconscious. Calas was dead. All because of him.

In the final moment, a vision filled Ezrah's mind.

* * *

I'm afraid.

Not of my weakness, but my power.

He always had been since that day, and suddenly, he was thrust back into a memory he'd been avoiding all his life.

Anna held his hand, standing over him, scrubbing her face of tears as the two were corralled by bandits and dragged out to the center square of the small town. There, bodies littered the ground. Half the homes were burning. The rest of the townsfolk sat huddled, dirty and crying, about a huge cart with a cage on its back. Two dozen bandits held blades. A fat bandit on a horse laughed as they neared, pointing to Ezrah, "Well, seems like you got yourself a pet." Then he eyed Ezrah's friends and neighbors, broken, huddled before the cart. "How many?"

"Two dozen. These are just the ones who didn't fight."

"What do we do with them, Horris?" asked the gaunt man that had cornered Ezrah and Anna, looking to the big man on the horse.

"Sell the women," Horris said with a cruel smile, sitting upon his mount, the sun glaring down, hiding his face. "After we've 'ad our fun, of course."

Another bandit asked, "What about the big man in the black keep? The Citadel won't take kindly to us in their backyard."

Horris guffawed, "You're afraid of the Patriarch? He and his little maggoty group of Reavers don't give a damn about this little dung heap of a town and its piss-poor peasants."

"What do we do with the rest of the sad lot?" asked another bandit.

Horris's eyes were full of malice. "Burn the town down. Kill the men and children."

The gaunt-faced scrawny man sighed but neared, raising a dagger to Ezrah, looming and blocking the sun. "So be it."

Ezrah could only stand there, stuck in his own fear, shuddering.

"No!" Anna shouted, running and covering him with her body. "You promised he'd be safe."

"Move aside, wench, or I'll run you through too," the man sneered.

Ezrah was crying, tears leaking down his face.

Anna stroked his cheek, wiping his tears. "Don't be afraid, Ez," she said, holding him. "It's going to be alright."

Another bandit came forward and ripped her away from him. Anna shouted and fought, being pulled towards the cart with a cage on it, and was thrown inside. The gaunt-faced man stepped forward, lifting his sword, and Anna continued to scream. Ezrah stood frozen. Rooted in fear. Why? Why wasn't he stronger? If only he was stronger...

"Sorry, little rat." The gaunt man's dagger descended.

If only he was stronger.

If only he was stronger.

His mother and father.

Anna.

His home.

All of it.

Ezrah's small body shook, not with fear suddenly, but with rage.

And power.

Ezrah roared, his small frame shaking with the immensity of it. The gaunt man stumbled back as something was streaming off Ezrah's body. Orange vapor. Spark. Ezrah cast titanic threads of fire. This time, the gaunt-faced man didn't have a chance to react. He was burnt to a crisp. The bandits standing behind were frozen in horror, and Ezrah turned his wrath upon them, fire shooting from his hands. Horris tried to flee, prodding his steed, only for flames to consume and turn him to ash. Ezrah's soul demanded more. Let it all burn. He lost himself to it, letting go of everything that was inside him.

Time fell away.

Hours or days later, a figure appeared over him, riding down the lonely dirt road.

Ezrah knelt in a huddled form, still sobbing.

The man had a rough face like the side of a cliff and a thick moustache. His cloak fluttered, showing a glimpse of an image of crossed swords. The Devari knelt, reaching out. "The name's Calas. What's yours?"

Ezrah was mute, stuck in his own horror, rocking back and forth.

Calas looked about at the mayhem, the houses now burnt to ash. Bodies all blackened. Just the silence of the dead. How much of it had been him and how much the bandits? Staring at his small hands, tears fell, wetting his dirty palms. So much fire from Ezrah's hands… A power to level mountains. He had done this. Calas's eyes seemed to understand. A terrible sorrow and weight crossed the big man's bluff face. "C'mon, lad. Shield your eyes now. It's time to go."

Ezrah scooted away, panicking.

Calas made calming words.

Ezrah stopped, and Calas smiled reassuringly. "Atta' boy. C'mon now." He picked him up gently, so kindly. He didn't deserve it. None of it. Ezrah continued to shake and sob. Calas's voice was a low soothing grumble as he held Ezrah, turning away, covering his eyes, "We're going to forget this place."

Ezrah saw through the slits of Calas's fingers as the town continued to smolder and burn.

It had been him.

✳   ✳   ✳

It was me.

Nalia stood over him.

"Don't be afraid anymore."

Words entered his head. *"Sometimes the power to do right requires the same power that can do wrong."*

He understood, and he summoned a breath, power roaring inside of him.

He opened his eyes, and as Nalia's power rushed over him, he grabbed her wrist. Ice coated it and snuffed her spell. Nalia shook her head. "No... I felt your spark, there was just a flicker left."

Ezrah rose to his feet and threw her, strengthening his arm with threads of flesh.

She flew, skidding across the ground.

Nalia picked herself up. "You don't even have the orb!"

Ezrah shook his head. "The orb was just a tool, a device to help me see what was already there."

69

She roared, "No! It should be me! I deserve to have the power of an Arbiter!"

"An Arbiter is more than power. They create, they give life, where you only take. No more," Ezrah said.

Nalia shook with power and sent fire out in all directions. Flames crawled up the walls, burning up the maze. Screaming, she directed the firestorm towards him.

Ezrah watched, feeling a mix of emotions. Rage, calm, tenacity, guile, empathy—all the elements swirled inside him, and he chose one. Letting go, he pulled from a deep source, a reservoir hidden beneath the land. The aqueducts. It bubbled forth, surging from the depths of Farhaven.

Water burst through the ground, quenching everything.

It surged upward, rising like a geyser, then came crashing back to earth. Nalia cried out in rage as the torrent smashed down upon her. Her writhing figure disappeared under the heavy downpour. Gods... He hadn't killed her, had he? No, not again. Nalia most definitely deserved death, but he couldn't become what he feared. Water was quickly filling the chamber.

Ezrah rushed to Fera's side, scooping her up.

Fera's clothes clung to her slender body, hair plastered to her ashen face, but she was still breathing. "Thank the gods," he uttered and looked about as water swelled around his feet, rising higher and higher, filling the maze. The altar could no longer be seen as the water rose to his ankles, then his knees. In the corner of his vision, there was a shifting of muscle. More geysers broke out, bursting forth from the depths of Farhaven, rising into the air.

At last, the waterfall washed out. Nalia stood in its place, surrounded by a barrier of molten flames. As he expected, it hadn't been enough. Now Ezrah hunted for a way out. Above the staircase, however, the door was shut. Even then, he'd never make it. In the looming roof above, there was a thin crack. Through it shone a ray of light. *Sunshine?*

Farbs...the streets of the city...

Nalia cackled. "A valiant attempt, little Neophyte. However, for all your power, you are still afraid to do what is necessary, aren't you?"

He snarled, "I won't become you."

A huge geyser burst nearby, sending a spray of water, and Nalia's eyes flickered to it. In that moment, as her gaze was transfixed, Ezrah sent out the magic of flesh. He had only enough time for a simple, rushed version of it, but he hoped it would be enough. Slowly, threads of flesh controlling the beast were dissolved like a small flame burning up a fuse. When the flame reached the end of the fuse, all the threads of flesh binding the creature would be no more.

Nalia advanced on them. The barrier of flames fell from her upper body and became a ring about her feet, like a blooming red rose, boiling and pushing back the water. Flames danced in her raised palm. "That's what you fear, isn't it? Your power. I feared it, too, but the only way forward is to give in to your rage, your hate. You have no choice, just like I didn't. To become strong, to gain true power, there is always a price to pay."

Fera, still covered in Calas's blood, was limp in Ezrah's arms. He felt the weight of the water pulling on her robes as it swelled around them. Backing up, he struggled to maintain his balance. "You're wrong!" He said, shaking his head, voice hoarse. "We always have a choice."

Still, she came closer, water hissing from her living shield of flames as she strode forth. Water rose higher and higher; up to his knees, the chamber would be flooded in no time. An animal snort sounded, but it was muted by the roar of water filling the chamber.

"Fool," Nalia cursed, only...for the first time, Ezrah saw sorrow in her eyes. As if she'd lost something dear to her. "The proof is in your very arms. If you don't have the wit to see it..." Nalia said, almost with resignation, a hesitancy, "then I will do what you can't and prove the price of power." Nalia's eyes became living orbs of hate, and she raised her hand and her bloody stump, casting monumental threads of fire.

Another roar sounded over the chamber's gushing water.

The minotaur rammed into Nalia like a two-ton draft horse.

Nalia flew three dozen feet, smashing into the maze's wall.

She twitched for a moment, her face still showing shock, then she went still, and her eyes glazed, her spark of life dimming like a coal with its last ember growing cold.

The beast's huge red muscles and tendons flexed as it turned on Ezrah and Fera. Ezrah flinched. The minotaur snorted and looked down at them, still gripping its bone axe. Issuing hot breaths, the beast took a step forward. Ezrah stared into its red eyes. As he did, he felt drawn in, as if looking into the creature's soul. It judged them for another long, tense moment. As if seeing what it needed to see, the minotaur gave a final snort and blessedly turned, walking into the flooded maze, leaving them alone.

"Seven hells," Ezrah said, catching his breath. Was it finally over?

More geysers burst all about. Water rose higher and higher, now up to his waist. It wasn't over yet. He'd dredged forth too much. The rising waters wouldn't, *couldn't* be stopped.

"Really wish you were here to call me a fool right now and help me out," he told Fera, who he cradled close.

A huge geyser erupted on his left, then on his right.

Ezrah was forced to swim, holding Fera's head above water. Still, the water level was rising higher and quicker. So he delved inward.

Using the spark glowing off of him, he formed a bubble of water around them both. He hardened it, making it swirl faster and faster until it fed off the water around them, a living ball of constant energy. It took everything he had. The ground rumbled, shaking with terrible power, and the biggest geyser yet erupted from the earth and smashed into Ezrah's sphere of water. He cried out as they were catapulted up

71

and out of the depths of the cavern, higher and higher. The water level rose faster and faster. The ceiling approached. Ezrah wrapped his arms around Fera and closed his eyes. "Hold on tight!"

The bubble, like a barrier of steel, burst through the roof of the cavern.

Bright light from the sudden sun assaulted his eyes. Ezrah let himself be expelled from the center of the hardened sphere of water, tumbling out like a piece of driftwood, still clutching onto Fera. Fera... Though he was tired and delirious from the sudden surge of power he'd just expended, Ezrah forced himself to move. Sopping wet, he dragged himself to his knees. Fera lay on the now wet desert ground. Her face was smooth, hair plastered to her face, looking so peaceful she almost could have been sleeping. Panicked, he felt her skin. It was clammy and cold. Fear seized him and Ezrah gripped her. "Fera!" She didn't move.

Then he realized she wasn't breathing.

No... he thought in horror.

Ezrah reached in, trying to pull the water from her lungs though his power was gone. He'd used every last ounce of spark to create the sphere of water. Now he cried out and pressed his hands onto her chest. Panic and terror overcame him. "Fera! Please! Gods, no, please!"

She was growing colder still, her skin ashen.

He cried out, shaking her and—

Fera coughed, spewing sudden water from her lungs. He sat, stunned, as Fera blinked at the bright sun and stared up at him, shielding her eyes. "Ez? What in the seven hells..."

"Oh, gods!" He embraced her tightly.

She groaned, "All right, all right, you're squeezing the air out of me, you big lummox. Hells, when did you get so strong?" He quickly let go, laughing and sitting back as Fera took in her surroundings. "Where... where are we? What happened?"

"I..." Then his words fell short.

Dazed, he heard voices. Shaking himself, he and Fera looked about to see citizens all around. They walked out from the desert streets, gazing in awe at something behind him and Fera. Ezrah turned and looked. In the center of a vast square in the desert streets of Farbs was a giant swirling sphere, suspended in midair and sustained by the geyser of water from below. Water soaked into the streets, turning the hard dirt to mud. Citizens rushed, filling buckets, crying out in joy. Other men and women moved to their side.

"The boy did it… He just appeared out of thin air surrounded by that…"

"Miracle." The whisper grew, eyes shining and looking down at him.

"Ez," Fera said, "what in the hells did you just do?" He shook his head, trying to find the words, staring up at the thing with her at his side. "Did you just make a Grand Creation?"

The giant orb of water continued to swirl, and Ezrah swallowed. "I think I did…"

A familiar face suddenly appeared out of the crowds. Grimwal. The big man smiled gruffly, then saw others crowding, getting closer. "Out of the way, you fools! Don't trample the boy!"

And Ezrah closed his eyes, letting it all go, hearing one final word. "*Arbiter…*" 73

* * *

Ezrah moved through the halls of the Citadel swiftly, his four-striped scarlet robes whisking across the cool black stone. An excited, nervous energy hung in the air. Servants, messengers, Reavers, Devari…all buzzed with the news of the prodigy's ascension. Not his, but Fera's.

For today, she'd rise to the rank of a four-stripe, matching him.

The Patriarch, leader of the Citadel, had deemed Arbiter a fitting title for Ezrah…if not yet. The wizened monarch's words returned. "*Upon your eighteenth birthday, you will fit the mantle that is yours by right. For now, you've still some things to learn.*"

Ezrah was more than alright with taking things slow.

Of course, that excited energy didn't banish all the shadows of the past. Like a sun rising upon a new day, a heaviness still clung. It had been two moons since the maze, the madness that was Nalia, and Calas's death. Ezrah's heart hurt. He missed Calas dearly, and he felt his mentor's absence in every corner of the keep. Farhaven was a little dimmer for it. Several Devari walked past wearing the full black cloth of mourning for their fallen leader.

However, despite Ezrah's heavy heart, today was a day of celebration. Fera. Suddenly, Ezrah spotted a familiar face. Reaver Sinistra. She still bore the three stripes. She bowed her head as he neared.

Ezrah almost passed her when he paused.

Reaver Sinistra stiffened as if ready to be struck. Her thin lips were pressed into a tight line, and her eyes tightened at the corners. Glancing up, she wondered why the long pause.

Ezrah sighed, and he lifted her chin.

"Reaver Ezrah?"

"I'm not Nalia, Reaver Sinistra."

She looked at him, confused and nervous.

Ezrah noticed others in the hall had stopped to watch the exchange. A tension held them all. So he raised his voice, this time for everyone in the hall to hear. "Things are going to change around here, starting with how we treat one another." Whispers sifted through the crowds, Neophytes and Reavers. "We are not so different, and we always have a choice. Remember that."

The general reaction to his words was varied.

Most seemed…confused. Others whispered excitedly as if he was about to summon another Grand Creation. Only one reaction interested him in that moment. Slowly, Reaver Sinistra raised her eyes to meet his. Her look of fear vanished, and she gave a slight nod. "Arbiter Ezrah," she said with a small smile. "I always knew you had potential in you."

Ezrah smiled back and continued on through the confused, whispering crowd.

Except there was *one* person that might still deserve a lesson. After all, he wasn't perfect.

So Ezrah made a quick side trip.

He entered the Neophyte Quarters and found Logan surrounded by his cronies, playing a game of elements in a hall with long glass tables. Upon his approach, there was a collective rush of silence. Logan's back was turned, snidely laying into his opponent, who was watching Ezrah approach. "Told you you were no good at this game, you lousy three-stripe." Logan snatched his opponent's glass bauble of fire from the board, and the flames on the figure were snuffed. "You're almost as bad as that—"

The others were pointing, whispering and gesturing behind Logan, but he was too consumed in his little victory. "What are you all yammering about? You—"

Ezrah said nothing.

Logan turned, saw Ezrah, and fell into a fit of stuttering.

Ezrah sighed. "I'll save you the trouble and get to the point. If I ever hear that you are hurting, bullying, or belittling other neophytes, I will personally turn you into a newt."

"Wait... Reavers can't do that, can they?" Logan said with a gulp.

Ezrah grinned and left them murmuring their speculations. He made his way towards the streets. He found Fera in her red robes where they'd planned to meet. She stood before the Water Sphere. It glistened magnificently. There was the sound of the constant trickle of water as it fed from the geyser below. Its iridescent curves rippled here and there, almost seeming otherworldly.

White stone streets radiated from the sphere, now a centerpiece of life and magic. Men and women thanked him as he neared, bowing and singing his praises.

Ezrah moved to Fera, falling in at her side, saying nothing.

She was silent, and he was content just being in her presence. He could see their distorted reflections in their water's rippling surface. Somehow, he hadn't noticed his height. He'd grown taller, almost lankier, and he saw the baby fat of his cheeks was hollowing out, showing cheekbones for once. His wild mat of hair was growing long too, almost to his shoulders now. He still had a scar on his forehead from where his shadow self had cut him with the moonblade. A subtle reminder to accept all parts of himself—his darkness and his light.

A bit of stubble was forming on his cheeks, chin, and upper lip, and he thought he might keep it, if only to make him look older; like one of those wise old Reavers out of the stories.

Fera, even in the shimmering reflection, looked immaculate. Her sleek black tresses now fell in perfect ringlets about her heart-shaped face. She stood tall as always, her posture perfect. Even her robes looked freshly pressed. Not a hair out of place. Their attire was what drew his eye. *Seven hells*, Ezrah thought, seeing their scarlet robes and four stripes.

They looked like legends. Well, young legends.

Together, they watched, as over the tops of the clay buildings, the sun set. It basked the city in rays of purple, orange, and even a sliver of green. It felt like twilight was setting on the old world, and a new one was dawning.

"You're quite proud of yourself, aren't you?" she asked without looking at him, mirroring her words from that day when he had helped break the barrels and slake the citizens' thirst.

"A little bit. Not half as proud as I am of you." He pinched her four-striped sleeves, wagging them in the air.

She snorted. "Come now, Reaver Ezrah, are you trying to make me embarrassed in public?"

Others watched them, giving them their space, content to fill their buckets. "Oh, wow, what formality." Ezrah rubbed his brow. "This is really going to go to your head, isn't it?"

She glanced at him smugly, violet eyes filled with mirth. "Going to? It already *has*. The Patriarch congratulated me, Ez. *The Patriarch*. Hells, I'm half expecting Renalin to float down on a mote of light and give me a pat on the back."

Ezrah made a strangled sound.

"You all right? Did I say something wrong?"

He hadn't told her of his vision. It felt private, personal… He was still processing his interaction with a being of light. He nodded, "No, nothing. I'm fine, just fine."

Fera grew serious, looking out at the streets, at the setting sun. "Everything's going to change now, isn't it?"

Ezrah watched as a little boy dipped a bucket into the sphere of water, and the hole reformed, complete once more. The boy ran back to his mother, laughing. "Yes," Ezrah said. "I think it is."

"Oh, I nearly forgot," Fera remarked suddenly. "I made this for you." She pulled out a little red box tied with a black ribbon.

"Fera… You know this is your day, not mine, right?"

"Exactly. That's why *I* get to do what *I* want. What I want is to give you a gift."

He groaned.

She shoved him playfully. "Just open it."

Ezrah pulled the ribbon free, and inside was a familiar twisting metal talisman.

The symbol of the Devari. The symbol of hope, honor, and courage. Just like the one Calas had given him. Identical in every way. It had been lost amid the chaos. He felt tears well as he stared at it, his vision going glassy.

Fera wrung her hands nervously. "Do you like it? I made it out of Yronia iron. It's just like yours." He gazed up at her and Fera shied her gaze, looking flustered. "Why are you looking at me like that? I'm sorry I lost it. I had plans to make one right away, but the iron cost me a pretty penny, so—"

Ezrah hugged her in a tight embrace, cutting short her rant. "It's perfect."

She released a heavy breath, easing into his embrace. "I'm so glad you like it. I was afraid you'd be mad."

"How could I?" Then he pulled away. "Except… Don't get mad, but there's just one thing wrong with it."

Her brows furrowed. "You just said it was perfect! If you're blaming my craftsmanship, Ez—"

Without speaking, Ezrah threaded metal and broke it in two. He placed half of the metal talisman in her palm. "So we can both feel each other's presence. Calas would have preferred it that way."

Fera's face lit with a smile, eyes watering.

Ezrah's grin mirrored her own, until he cleared his throat, looking about at the milling crowds.

"Right, anyway," Fera said, wiping tears, "did you invite me out here on my day of celebration just to gloat?"

"Hardly. I was parched." Then he gestured to a nearby inn over the heads of people. "Shall we? I hear they have a desert pear cider that's quite exquisite."

Spotting the inn's sign, Fera rolled her eyes. "Your treat, I'm guessing?"

He gave an elaborate bow, extending his hand. "Of course, Reaver." With that, he escorted Fera across the lively square, towards the inn, its swinging sign painted black with gold lettering reading: *An Arbiter's Gift.*

* * *

ACKNOWLEDGEMENTS

To my mother. My rock, my confidant, and the one who always encouraged me (and still does) to follow my passion.

79

80

ABOUT THE AUTHOR

MATTHEW WOLF was born on March 14, 1986, in Southern California.With the combination of a great deal of solitude, breathtaking landscapes from world travel, and a heap of books, Matt began The Ronin Saga at the age of eighteen. Other inspirations include studying martial arts and practicing for five years as a Kung Fu and Tai Chi instructor. His various hobbies may or may not include duck herding, extreme ironing, and making snow globes.

He now writes out of his home in California where, while crafting worlds of magic, he often forgets to eat. If he's not writing, Matthew tours comic conventions, schools, libraries, and bookstores to spread the word of the Ronin.

www.matt-wolf.com